THE ONLY WAY OUT

A bully, a victim and a bystander whose lives will never be the same.

KATIE KUPERMAN

THIS BOOK IS DEDICATED TO

My two incredible children.
May you never feel the wrath of a bully, and if you do, may
you know the way out.

Amanda Todd.
A life too short. Without your story, I never would have put
pen to paper. Rest in peace.

THE STORY BEHIND THE STORY

Though I always knew I wanted to write a book, I was never certain about the subject matter…until I became aware of Amanda Todd's story. A young teen who described her experience as one of struggle, bullying and self-harm, Amanda's life ended tragically in suicide at the age of 15. It is her story that inspired me to write *The Only Way Out*.

When it came time to publish, I was consumed by a strong desire to acknowledge Amanda's name. I sought out Carol Todd, Amanda's mother and a prominent voice in the bullying prevention space. She granted me permission and now I am truly honored to have this book dedicated to Amanda.

Since then, Carol Todd and I have connected in a few ways, one of which is a donation partnership. A portion of the proceeds from every book sale of *The Only Way Out* will be donated to the Amanda Todd Legacy Society, which makes a direct impact through education, awareness and support for those who struggle with bullying and mental health issues.

THE ONLY WAY OUT

CONTENTS

1

MOTIONLESS

I stood there and watched. It was horrible. They beat her right there in the schoolyard. Utterly ashamed yet too much of a coward to make a move, I hid behind the trunk of our school's oldest tree.

Fear paralyzed me.

As I watched this ghastly incident take place right before my eyes, I desperately wondered how we got here. How had our lives come to this? There I was, hiding, weak and petrified. And there was my dearest Rebecca, lying, still and lifeless.

Why wasn't I stronger? Why couldn't I be the brave one to save her? One of us had to be – and yet none of us were. An evil had taken over our school and if you were on the unlucky side of it, you didn't stand a chance. The longer I stood there, the more frightened I became.

I saw the crowd around her disperse, but Rebecca didn't move. There was blood. My breath quickened as I realized the severity of the situation. In my mind, I begged for a physical gesture – for a sign that she was okay.

Nothing.

What had they done?!

Three teachers rushed the field. As they flooded the space around her, I felt myself begin to walk forward. Every so often, I'd catch a glimpse of Rebecca between the movement as people scrambled on their cell phones and frantically shouted over and over again, "Call 911! Call 911!"

Slow and robotic, I forced myself to walk. In that moment, I experienced the crippling sensation of my most haunting, recurrent dream. The one in which I needed desperately to run fast but it was as though a force much greater held me back. I could feel my face wincing in pain and frustration as I tried to be quick. But the fear was too great. It overtook me and my entire body began to shake. In one moment, I heard the screams – the panic – among the students and teachers who stood above her, and in the next, nothing but my own deep, panting breath.

The fire truck arrived. Already? I wondered how long I'd been frozen in my own slow-motion reality. Now I stopped dead in my tracks as I watched the firefighters blast the scene. I couldn't see Rebecca at all anymore.

An ambulance pulled in.

Then another fire truck.

Then two police cars.

After what felt like only seconds, I saw two men in uniforms emerge from the crowd, holding Rebecca on a stretcher. A large lump formed in my throat. I tried to swallow it away but it wouldn't budge, making my breath quicken to a pace that began to terrify me. I was losing control.

Step. I tried to instruct my legs to move.

Step. I tried again.

Gasping for breath, body shaking, knees buckling, somehow I made it. I reached that tainted spot on the field. Stopping dead in my tracks, I stared at the ground beneath my feet. The patch of grass where she had lain was tousled and matted and now had a different consistency than the rest of the field. You could tell something happened there. Everything grew blurry as my eyes welled with tears.

2

ON OUR WAY

"Don't forget your lunch!" Mom screeched. My goodness was she ever nervous. Her voice always echoed the same high-pitched tone whenever she was anxious about something.

"I won't," I replied, trying to keep my voice calm so she wouldn't sense my own strong sentiment of anticipation. That would only make matters worse. I smiled at her as she continued to bustle about all around me. It was a big day! Her "little girl" (although I despised the thought of that expression since I was a whopping fourteen now) was growing up – much too fast if you asked her. But Mom's emotions didn't hinder my mood in the slightest – I was so excited I could barely contain myself! A new school, new people, new classes, new teachers… Slightly nerve racking I suppose and I'm sure every ninth grader's mind was buzzing uncontrollably with similar questions: Will I fit in? Will people like me? Will I get good grades? Will I have nice teachers?

As I took one last look at myself in the large hall mirror, Dad piped up from the living room behind me, "All ready, Kiddo?"

"Ready as I'll ever be," I said. To be honest, I just wanted to get the first day over with! The summer buildup was too much to bear a moment longer.

I imagine I was a great deal more nervous than other students because the only other person I knew was my best friend and next-door neighbor, Rebecca. You see, Leacrest High was an arts school with specialty programs for drama, visual arts, music and dance. Students who lived within the specified surrounding area could attend Leacrest without a focus in the arts, whereas those who were accepted into the arts program were permitted to attend the high school even though they resided outside the mainstream boundaries. Rebecca and I were out-of-area arts students (she in music and I in dance), which meant that unlike other grade nines we wouldn't have the vast majority of our elementary school friends with us. Although I was slightly apprehensive about the fact that literally every last one of my previous schoolmates was attending a different school, I was thrilled to be with Rebecca at last. We'd always attended different elementary schools but had become the best of friends over the last twelve years as next-door neighbors.

I gave Dad a big hug, kissed Mom on the cheek and made my way out the front door. I took a deep breath. The air outside was fresh and I felt it flow through my nostrils, past my throat and into my chest. I walked across the porch towards Rebecca's house. Our families had arranged that her father would drive us to school, since it was on the way to his office. I couldn't have been happier about the plan because it meant one less city bus ride for us.

As I jumped off the porch, walked across the grass and onto Rebecca's driveway, I could feel my parents staring at me through the living room window. I chuckled a little to myself and turned around to verify my suspicion. Yes, there they were, now smiling and waving frantically. I laughed even harder as I waved back.

Continuing across the driveway to the Blaines' doorstep, I felt my nerves begin to subside. Before I even had a chance to knock, Rebecca swung the door open and greeted me with an excited scream.

"Can you believe it?" she squealed.

"I know. This is crazy!" I yelled as we linked arms down the walkway.

Mr. Blaine was only a mere second behind us and he almost startled me as he grabbed my shoulders, gave them a little shake and asked excitedly, "Ready for your first day, Kaitlyn?"

"You bet, Mr. Blaine," I replied. "Especially since I have Rebecca here with me."

"Yeah, it's fantastic you gals get to do this together," he said as he opened the car door and plunked inside. I nestled into the back seat while Rebecca took the front. I felt the car jolt as Mr. Blaine shifted into reverse.

Rebecca was a talented saxophone player. We'd lived next door to one another nearly our entire lives. When each of us was just a year old, the Blaines and my parents moved into numbers 12 and 14 Buckingham Way, respectively.

The dearest of friends we were – sharing similar interests, enjoying highly entertaining play dates and always spending as much time together as possible. During our elementary years, Rebecca attended a French immersion school in our local town and I a public school. And now finally the time had come. We'd be together.

As young children we took turns at each of our homes, flipping from one house to another, playing in each other's basements, swimming in the Blaines' pool, conducting intense baking sessions in my parents' kitchen and building secret hideaways in each other's backyards.

"Taste Tests" were my favorite. Actually, I could never quite decide whether I hated the game or loved it. The designated setting was the kitchen, and back and forth, we'd take turns.

"You're up!" Rebecca would say, her hands wrapped tightly 'round her back.

"Ugh! I don't want to," I'd whine, a huge grin on my face. We'd burst into hysterical laughter, each of us sharing the same undecided, love-hate sentiment for the game.

"C'mon now, it's only fair," Rebecca would insist.

I'd close my eyes and purse my lips shut.

"Open up," she'd demand.

Frowning and pursing my lips shut at first, I'd finally decide to slowly open my mouth. Again, my laughter would get the better of me and I'd fall over in my chair as Rebecca frantically stepped backwards to hide her arms yet again behind her back so as not to spoil the surprise of whatever tasty – or maybe not so tasty – treat awaited me. Sometimes our bouts of hysterical laughter would continue on for quite some time until finally we'd gain our composure long enough for me to taste whatever it was she held so secretively behind her back.

I'd open my mouth as wide as I could and the spoon would enter. "Now close," Rebecca would order. I'd close my mouth and slowly begin swishing my tongue around, usually with a disgusted look on my face. What was most unnerving was this very part of the game – feeling a foreign texture and taste in my mouth, and then trying desperately to figure out what it was. After a few seconds, I'd have it! My expression would turn from disgust to utter pleasure.

"Peanut butter and chocolate sauce!" I'd exclaim. "Phew!"

Again, we'd laugh. Always respectful of one another, the object of the game was not to make one another ill, but rather to enjoy a tasty treat and guess what it was. You'd be surprised how many times neither one of us could decipher what strange substance was floating around in our mouths! I'm sure if we were boys, the game would have taken on a much different form. Maybe Tabasco sauce mixed with strawberry jam?

When Rebecca and I came to the conclusion that we would both audition for the arts programs at Leacrest High School, we knew there'd be several nerve-racking months ahead of us. Although at first I presumed the auditions would be the worst of it all, I couldn't have been more wrong. The most terrifying part of the process was the waiting – the long, tedious, cannot-stand-another-moment period of anticipation before the response letters were mailed.

We spoke about it often and Rebecca was just as apprehensive as I – not only for her own admittance into the school, but for mine too. How awful it would have been if only one of us had made it! Thank goodness we were both selected.

Or so I thought.

Today, I wish with all my heart that Rebecca hadn't been accepted to Leacrest High.

3

THE FIRST DAY

When I first rolled out of bed, I knew they were there but I did my best to ignore them – now, the butterflies invading my stomach fluttered about so fast it felt as though thousands of small winged animals were going to escape right through my skin at any moment. I couldn't possibly disregard them any longer. Trying to control myself, I thought back to what I was taught during a sports psychology session in gymnastics: "nerves are the result of a chemical response in the body characterized by excess energy and it is up to you to decide whether or not you let them get the best of you or use them to your advantage".

I slowly stepped out of Mr. Blaine's car and stared at the front entrance of what would be my school – my home base – for the next four years.

Leacrest High had a far more aesthetically pleasing appearance than other high schools. Instead of your typical, uninteresting red or beige brick, the school's exterior was made of a shimmering, colorful, square-shaped material that was complimented by white, stone-like paneling. Rumor has it the structure was originally built as a shopping mall, not a high school.

I wasn't sure the reason for the change, but perhaps this could explain its undoubtedly unique appearance. To my right, was the school's theater. Although it was also used for public purposes, the Leacrest Theater was the high school's dedicated venue for shows and events throughout the school year. As a dancer in the arts program, I was sure to become well acquainted with it in no time.

I heard Rebecca say goodbye to her father and I turned around to do the same. She closed the passenger door, tightly linked her arm with mine and exclaimed, "This is it!"

I smiled back nervously. Despite my attempts to hide it, I suppose my anxiousness was apparent because she went on confidently, "Don't worry, Kaitlyn. It's going to be fun. We've got each other."

"You're right," I answered. Why was I so nervous? Maybe it's because I've always had a strong desire for social approval – not in the sense that I ever felt the need to be someone I wasn't or to act in a way that made me feel uncomfortable, but actually quite the opposite. All my life, no matter where I was, who I was with or what I was doing, I seemed to fit in – naturally. I was outgoing, friendly and confident – the kind of kid you could bring anywhere and not worry. Within minutes, I'd be fluttering about the crowd, meeting new people and enjoying various conversations. When I was with family, I felt loved. When I was at school, the girls were my friends and the boys liked me. Even when I first joined my dance studio, I was the new girl entering what was clearly already a tightly knit group of girls and yet, I was quickly accepted and even adored. I was such an extroverted social addict, that the thought of my high school experience being anything but collective was impossible. And yet now I'd been stripped of my elementary friendships and was about to walk into a school of about two thousand students where the only one I knew was standing right next to me. Just because I'd enjoyed the excitement and self-affirmation of a popular existence up until now, didn't mean high school would mirror that. It could very well be the opposite. Still, my nerves didn't add up.

As I think back, the truth is clear. Of course, I felt apprehensive walking into an entirely new phase of life, vulnerable and alone. But that wasn't all: the nerves I felt weren't only for me, they were also for Rebecca. Although she and I got along like two peas in a pod, we were fundamentally different from one another. I wouldn't go so far as to say she was shy, but certainly cautious, discreet and somewhat introverted, and even though it wasn't overly discernible, I sensed that she was insecure. As I tell my story, now it's quite obvious to me: my stomach churned for my dear friend too – not just for myself. What would she be faced with on the receiving end of our high school? If I knew the answer to that question in the moments when Rebecca and I walked with linked arms towards that place we called high school, I would have done everything in my power to block her way.

Rebecca reached for the door handle and we marched through the entrance side by side, giggling as our shoulders pressed together awkwardly between the doorframe. The main entrance took us into what appeared to be the second floor of the school and just ahead of us was a large dou-ble-sided staircase which led to the first floor down below. The bellowing voices and loud commotion told us that down those very stairs was where we wanted to go. As my head turned from one side to the other, I tried to take it all in. The architecture certainly resembled that of a shopping mall since you could actually gaze downwards from the second and third floors to the center, first-floor atrium area. The second level reminded me of a balcony, completely open with a half-wall barrier you could lean against to enjoy a full view of the action on the first floor. The third floor was similar, but it had glass encasements all around it (I assumed for safety reasons).

The air smelled of freshly baked muffins. The scent was so intoxicat-ing, it felt as though I could actually taste the pungent flavors without even a morsel in my mouth. My stomach growled loudly and I couldn't quite make out whether it was hunger pains or anxiousness. We approached the central staircase and took our first descending steps. Both of us shifted our focus to the left, where several groups of friends huddled in different areas throughout the cafeteria. Cliques already, I thought to myself.

The central staircase formed a landing close to the bottom, which then broke off to the left and right – the right leading into one of the locker areas and the left into the cafeteria. Rebecca and I shifted to the left.

"Where do you want to sit?" I asked.

"I think before we sit down we should get one of those deli-cious-smelling muffins," Rebecca replied.

"Ha! You read my mind. I was just thinking about that amazing smell as we were walking down the stairs."

We took the last few steps towards the cafeteria doors but were sud-denly halted close to the opening. A rather large lineup had formed. I sup-pose everyone else had the same idea we did.

"Watch it!" the tall girl ahead of us snarled, looking directly at Rebecca.

"Sorry," Rebecca answered sheepishly, appearing quite stunned.

Despite the compassionate and apologetic nature of Rebecca's response, the girl continued to stare. Looking Rebecca up and down in a judgmental, condescending manner, the hateful stranger rolled her tongue over her teeth. After swiftly flashing an evil glance in my direction, she turned around to face the line in front of her.

Rebecca and I slowly turned our heads towards one another and shared a look of alarm. Rebecca's face was flush with embarrassment and my heartbeat quickened as my nerves escalated. As much as I could tell how badly we each wanted to exchange our take on the confusing encoun-ter that had just taken place, we most certainly couldn't with her standing right in front of us! Thank goodness our awkward moment was masked by the hustle and bustle of the cafeteria.

As I stood there burning a hole into the back of her head, a whirl of anger swept over me. The nerve of this girl! Who did she think she was? All too aware of the fact that I was completely detached from my comfort zone, at once this startling incident made me intimidated and vulnerable. If this were elementary school, it would have never even occurred to me to take the silent, cowardly route. But here, fists clenched and muscles tense, I knew it was the wiser move.

Her hair was long and streaked with a mix of platinum blond and chestnut brown colors in thick, dominant strips. Most other girls' highlights were pencil thin, but the hair on the head directly in front of me made a much bigger statement. It draped over the hood of her beige-colored rain jacket and fell loosely over the sides. It was slightly tangled, as though she'd forgotten to brush it that morning – or, what was likely more accurate, she didn't care. She wore dark blue skinny jeans tucked into black combat-style boots and draped over her left shoulder was a black bag, with the corner of a notebook protruding out of the back corner. Leaning into her left hip with her head tilted, eyes down on her smartphone and right leg extended far out to the side, our confrontational stranger oozed confidence. Maybe she was a senior. Yes, of course, she must be. Surely no new grade-nine would have had the guts to do what she did on the very first day of school.

My assumption made me feel better already. Snarky seniors always tried to prove their rule over the school – it was the same in elementary. I sighed a breath of relief. As the line began to move forward, the girl quickly ducked to the left and disappeared into the crowd inside the cafeteria doors. Once I was positive she was gone, I grabbed Rebecca's arm and immediately turned my attention towards her.

"What the hell was that?!" I demanded.

Her hand over her chest, Rebecca released a huge breath now that her instigator had fled the scene. "I guess we moved into line so fast, that when it suddenly stopped, my arm nudged the back of her," Rebecca explained.

"I didn't even see that!" I replied in disbelief. "It couldn't have been that big of a shove."

"Honestly," Rebecca went on, "I barely touched her."

"She was just looking to make a statement on the first day," I said, confident with the logic I'd construed in my mind just a moment before. "I'm sure she's a senior – or in any case, not a grade nine."

"Yeah," Rebecca responded, seemingly pleased with my interpretation.

"Don't sweat it," I assured her. "There's one in every school."

She smiled nervously. We took a few minutes to familiarize ourselves with the cafeteria, our eyes scanning one side and then the other. The smell of freshly baked muffins was even stronger now and we made our way towards the pile in a basket on the left. I reached a hand out, "Oh, they're still warm," I said, my mouth watering. I chose carrot and Rebecca, banana. We made our way to the cash register, paid and exited. By the time we made it out into the seating area we took one look at the clock on the wall and realized we were out of time.

"8:25 already," Rebecca muttered.

"Yeah, unfortunately. Let's go. I'm on the third floor, what about you?"

"Second," she answered.

We walked together up the center staircase and bid our farewells as she continued down the second-floor hallway and I circled around to the right to catch the next flight of stairs. It hadn't been an entirely smooth start, but it was nothing to fret about, I reassured myself. At the top of the final flight of stairs, I pulled my schedule out from my jacket pocket to double check the room number of my first class. I shoved the schedule back in my pocket as I made my final steps to the classroom and walked through the door.

The teacher stood at the front, scribbling something on the chalkboard. I walked towards the middle of the room and settled my eyes on a desk – not too far front and not too far back. Perfect. As I walked towards my decided home base, my gaze shifted upwards to the row at the back. My heart dropped into my stomach.

There she sat.

Our morning perpetrator.

I slouched into my chair and faced the front of the room. What?! She was in grade nine! Or had she flunked this class? That would perhaps partly explain her repugnant attitude. Heart racing and hands shaking I couldn't believe my horrible luck. I'd be forced to share a classroom with this terrible girl for the entire semester!

"Hey you!"

I heard the raspy, aggressive, yet all too familiar voice call out from behind me. For a split second, I debated whether or not to turn around. I could play the ignorance card…pretend I thought she was calling for someone else. Yes, good plan. Maybe she'd give up. Trying my best to look busy, I pulled my bag off my shoulder and placed it on the desk in front of me. I began to reach inside for my binder when…

"Helloo-ooo!" the voice came again, this time in a higher pitch with greater authority and it was accompanied by a startling knock to the shoulder. Stunned, I jumped in my seat and quickly whipped myself around. As she slowly retracted her arm, I noticed the pen in her hand – clearly her "tapper" of choice. I said nothing and put on my most confident face.

All lips and no teeth, she grinned devilishly and remarked, "You're the one who was with that girl who bumped into me outside the caf."

"It was an accident you know, you didn't have to make such a big deal of it," I replied, wickedly impressed with how self-assured I sounded.

She raised her eyebrows high in disbelief. It was as though this was the very first time she'd heard someone talk back to her. My heart raced faster and I felt something awful coming my way. Her eyebrows lowered to their usual place just above her eyes and she shrugged her shoulders nonchalantly. "Whatever," she snapped. "Someone bumps into me, you damn well better believe I'm gonna say something."

"Haven't you ever bumped into anyone before?" I asked as calmly as I could, desperately trying to prove my point to defend my friend.

"No!" she replied sarcastically, the evil grin returning to her face.

Ignoring her sarcasm, I retorted, "So maybe next time put yourself in the other person's shoes before you act like that for no reason!" Maybe that was too far. It dawned on me that the last thing I wanted to do was create enemies on the first day of school. I made a conscious decision to say no more. But then, something unexpected happened.

"Ha ha!" she laughed aloud. "I like you. What's your name?"

I couldn't believe what I was hearing. "Kaitlyn," I responded, my voice firm. I hadn't exactly warmed to her the way she had to me.

"I'm Chantel," she said.

Although relieved that this little encounter hadn't escalated into a bigger matter, truthfully, I didn't care to know her name. I was certainly more than eager to make friends but not with someone like this. Thankfully, there was no time to respond. Behind me I heard the all-too-familiar sounds of the classroom: the clap of the chalk as it made its descent into the metal tray down below, and the hissing of two hands rubbing together as they shook the unwanted residue.

"Okay everyone," a deep voice bellowed, friendly yet authoritative. "Welcome to Leacrest High School. This is Grade 9 English and my name is Mr. Kemp."

I spun back around to face the front of the classroom and reached inside my bag for my binder – this time, without interruption. I wondered what could account for Chantel's poor behavior. Bad parenting? An unpleasant home life? A traumatic incident that had hardened her? Such a large chip she carried on her shoulder...

I shook my head as if to end my current train of thought – an endless trail of wonderment I knew would only be a colossal waste of time. Besides, this was my very first class of high school! It was supposed to be enlightening and exciting – not tainted by the rough-edged girl behind me.

The day flew by and before long, it was time for Rebecca and I to embark on our first bus ride back home. Although many of the school's out-of-area arts students had dedicated yellow buses to take them to and from the institution, we were not so privileged. For whatever reason, our town was *not* included in the school's transportation route, and thus, we were left to battle public transit. We planned to catch the bus at a local stop just across the main road to the south of the high school and then transfer at the shopping mall close to our homes for the final trek.

Our meeting spot was the main cafeteria and we'd walk to the stop together from there. I sat at one of the weathered, blue cafeteria tables and awaited my partner in crime. Linking eyes from across the way, we smiled at one another and I began to gather my things.

"So?" Rebecca asked inquisitively.

"One down, like a million more to go," I smirked. "How are your classes?"

"They're good!" Rebecca responded, with her usual spunk and enthusiasm. It appeared as though the early morning's altercation was the furthest thing from her mind. "I especially enjoy my art class and I feel good about my English teacher too."

English! The moment she said the word, my mind flooded with Chantel's raspy voice hollering out from behind me. Should I tell Rebecca? She seemed so excited about her first day and I didn't want to be the cause of a negative change in her disposition but I simply couldn't hold it in.

"Who's your English teacher?" I questioned.

"Mr. Kemp, I think his name is," she replied.

"Oh! Me too! He seems nice, doesn't he? A voice I could listen to for hours..." I said, remembering his deep and commanding tone. "But you'll never guess –" I flashed her a weighty look.

"What?"

"That awful girl from this morning's cafeteria line is *in* my English class!"

"Ugh, seriously?" Rebecca sounded genuinely disappointed and almost sympathetic of the fact that I'd be forced to share a classroom with such a rotten individual.

"Yup. Brutal, right?"

"Did she recognize you? Did she say anything?"

"As a matter of fact, she did!" I exclaimed, diving right into my story. "Her name is Chantel and I tried so hard to ignore her but she sat diagonally behind me, called out to me and then when I didn't answer tapped my shoulder with her pen! You'll be happy to know I stood up for you, though. Even gave her a piece of my mind, actually."

"Oh, yeah?" Rebecca replied, seeming quite impressed.

"But then she said she *liked* me!" I shouted disgustedly. "I think because I gave her attitude or something. She must think I'm a bully like her."

"Ugh," Rebecca sounded revolted by the thought. "Well, don't become friends with her or anything."

We both chuckled at the ridiculous thought.

Rebecca held open the back door of the cafeteria, allowing me to walk through first. The crisp afternoon air sent a chill through my body. The sky was clear blue, speckled with a few wispy clouds, and even though the sun shone brightly, the briskness in the air reminded me that fall was just around the corner. As we walked across the lush green field towards the bus stop, we shared first-day stories: who we'd met, what our teachers were like, how much we'd enjoyed the freshly baked muffins in the morning and, in general, the excitement we felt for the many high school years that loomed ahead. I was relieved to see that Rebecca seemed unaffected by Chantel. Her positive attitude helped me put it all to rest in my own head.

As we rounded the last bend towards our street, we made plans to watch a movie together that night. Neither of us had been inundated with homework just yet and we decided to take advantage. We bid our farewells as I walked up the drive to my house and she to hers. I slid my key into the slot and slowly opened the front door. I couldn't wait to share my first day with Mom and Dad.

4

IF IT GOES UP, DOES IT ALWAYS COME DOWN?

His hair was blond, thick and wavy. The kind that was just long enough for you to coolly run your hands through – something he did a lot. About five foot eight, he stood tall above me, but certainly wouldn't have been considered *tall*. And I liked that. We shared math class together and just happened to sit adjacent to one another on the second day only to find out at the end of class that those would become our permanent seats for the year. Even though I learned later that he had a number of friends at the school, it just so happened that none of them were in this class, which I think is most of the reason why he and I began talking to one another in the first place.

Our connection began at the end of class, just after Ms. Singh informed us of our permanent seating arrangement. As everyone looked around themselves on all sides to evaluate whether or not they were pleased with the announcement, Jacob and I coincidentally locked eyes. We each chuckled awkwardly and he spoke first, "Guess we're stuck being neighbors then."

I giggled flirtatiously, "Could be worse." He seemed to like my response because I could feel him staring at me as I packed up my bag.

"I'm Jacob," he grinned.

"Kaitlyn," I answered back hastily. As I looked into his eyes, at once I felt the attraction. He was good-looking, but not in an arrogant way – in the humble, oblivious kind of way that every girl looks for but that few actually find. I felt my stomach flutter with excitement.

We exited class together and began walking down the hall towards the cafeteria. "So, how's your first week?" he asked.

"Good! How about you?"

"Pretty good…it doesn't really feel all that different since most of my buddies from elementary came here too."

"Oh really? See, I'm in the complete opposite position. None of my elementary school friends are here and I only know one other girl, who's my next-door neighbor, actually. So, I take it you live in the area?" I asked, looking over at him as we walked.

"Yeah, I can walk here in about five minutes. Do you come from far way?"

"Not too far, but it certainly isn't a five-minute walk! I live east about 15 minutes. It's okay in the morning because we get a ride from my friend's dad, but after school we have to take public transit," I replied, pursing my lips and scrunching my nose in displeasure.

"Oh, that sucks," he said, chuckling, and I slapped his shoulder teasingly. "You must be in one of the arts programs, then."

"Yeah, dance."

"Ohhhh, a dancer," he flirted back with an impressed look on his face. I smiled as I felt my cheeks flush.

"So, where you headed now? I have my spare actually…meeting up with a few buddies in the caf."

"Oh, it's my spare too," I said.

"Oh yeah?" he answered, "Come, I'll introduce you to the guys. We need a girl around to balance us out anyway," he joked.

As we made our way through the crowds and into the cafeteria, I noticed him scouring the tables for his friends. "Oh, there they are, c'mon!"

Three guys sat at the table, laughing hysterically among themselves as though one of them had just told the most hilarious story.

"Hey guys!" Jacob shouted as we approached.

"Hey man," they each chimed in.

"This is Kaitlyn," Jacob introduced me.

I shook each of their hands and felt my face grow hot. It was a little intimidating sitting down at a table full of guys I'd never met, but I enjoyed it nevertheless. I'd always been somewhat of a "guy's girl" – the drama that plagued the vast majority of girls my age was unbearable and I often found myself longing for more time with guys like Jacob and his friends. Guys seemed so much more down to earth, straightforward – no nonsense, no cattiness. I'd been the only girl in many scenarios at my previous school and even at family gatherings where the only "kids" at the party were my four male cousins and I. To be honest, I was always happiest in these types of situations – I could be myself, enjoying lighthearted conversations, jokes and good times.

I sat down and gradually settled in at the table. It didn't take long for the questions to begin. Where did I live? Did I know anyone else at the school? How did I like Leacrest so far? Did I have any other girlfriends I could introduce to them? Not to my surprise, the moment Jacob spilled the beans about the fact that I was in the dance program, the friendly interrogations really took off. The guys seemed nice. Funny as hell. I'm pretty sure

I was laughing hysterically for at least three quarters of my spare period, and when the time came for us to go our separate ways to the next class, I was delighted by an invitation that came my way.

Malik, the one with short, dark hair spoke casually, "Hey, Kaitlyn, I'm throwing kind of a school kickoff party this weekend. You should come!"

"Sounds awesome!" I replied excitedly with not so much as a second's hesitation. "Can I bring my friend, Rebecca, I was telling you about?"

"For sure!"

And then, something even more wonderful happened…

"Why don't you give me your number and I'll text you Malik's address and everything," Jacob suggested.

I was elated. Smooth, clever and yet clearly an indication that maybe he liked me. Right? Over the course of our spare period, as much as I grew fond of his friends, Malik, Ryker and Noah, my high school crush had most certainly settled on Jacob.

I smiled at him, "Perfect."

We said goodbye to the other guys and they disappeared into the now bustling crowds as the two of us hung back for a moment to exchange numbers.

"What floor you going to?" I asked.

"Uh, third I think."

"Okay, let's go, I'm on the second this period."

We walked together up the stairs and said our goodbyes in front of my class. It was the perfect meeting. He was painstakingly good-looking, kind, funny, genuine…had I just hit the high school dating jackpot?

Needless to say, over the next few weeks I was distracted. *Very* distracted. I quickly fell in love with my dance program, my classes were far more exciting than elementary school, and I seemed to have been adopted with open arms into a large group of friends that just so happened to include my high school crush. Throughout the next few weeks following our first meeting, Jacob and I talked on the phone, texted between classes, sometimes hung out in the caf after school and attended parties on the weekends. Our relationship grew deeper and we quickly fell into a comfortable pattern.

I was so happy with the new group of friends I'd made that I wanted nothing more than for Rebecca to join me in all the excitement. I invited her to spend time with us after school, prompted her to attend weekend gatherings and constantly reminded her of all the good-looking boys Jacob was friends with. But to my surprise, she repeatedly declined. It wasn't due to disinterest, but rather segregation. You see, as I was busy meeting my crush and willingly stepping my way knee deep into his circle of friends, Rebecca was forming her own high school relationships. We had not a single class in common and so, quite naturally I suppose, we had but a single common friend: just one guy by the name of Marcel who I shared science with and Rebecca, math. It wasn't deliberate, it wasn't intentional and neither one of us felt abandoned by the other. This was simply a natural process, and although it was the last thing we ever thought would happen, it marked the beginning of our journey apart.

How thrilled we'd been to *finally* attend the same school together. All summer long we'd talked about how incredible our new experience would be and how we'd become even closer friends with so many new things to share. But our predictions could not have been more misguided, for now, here we were, not more than a few weeks in, and the only time we saw each other was during morning car rides with Mr. Blaine and occasionally the afternoon bus ride home. And as a matter of fact, those times were always enjoyable. We'd learn about one another's lives, catch up, share a good laugh and then go our separate ways.

By early October, Jacob and I had become "official". I was completely consumed by him. He made me feel good about myself in a way that no one else ever had and he seemed to love every side of me – artistic, fun, goofy, sarcastic, serious, intense…it didn't matter. I adored his personality, his demeanor, his attitude… It was the happiest time of my entire high school experience and it was at this point that I often thought to myself, there's no way it can get any better than this.

Turns out I was right.

5

SHE WAS DIFFERENT

It was October 20th. I snatched my bag, grabbed my coat and threw on the very first pair of shoes I laid eyes on at the front door. I hollered a quick farewell to Mom and Dad over my shoulder and ran outside to the Blaines. As I swung open the back door to Mr. Blaine's car and plunked myself clumsily into the seat, I apologized profusely for my tardiness that morning.

"Not a problem," Mr. Blaine chuckled. "Rebecca seemed a little on the slower side today too."

"Oh really?" I remarked, instantly relieved.

"I was slower because I'm sick," Rebecca's voice was rash and filled with frustration. I'd never heard her speak to her father in such a way.

"We spoke about this already, Rebecca," Mr. Blaine confirmed. "You're not ill enough to miss school."

Rebecca scowled at her father, her arms clasped tightly in front of her chest. She shifted her body to face forward again as she let out a deep sigh. This was a side of Rebecca of which I'd seen very little. She certainly didn't *sound* sick. Perhaps there had been an incident with her parents that morning and if so, I knew she'd offload every juicy detail the moment we were out of the car, but for the next fifteen minutes, there was only silence. I felt my body loosen as the gentle bobbing motion of the car shook away my morning stress. I gazed out the window, watching every home, tree and side street fly by as we made our way to our destination. It didn't take long before I'd forgotten the awkwardness of the silence and instead, embraced it. Life was always inundated with noise and it was nice to enjoy a few moments of quiet. The sound of the car engine hummed soothingly in the background, making it even easier for me to relax and empty my mind of what was usually filled with a sea of endless, entangled thoughts. As I slipped into an even deeper state of relaxation, I became further disconnected from the world around me. Just as fast as I'd fallen in, I was abruptly pulled out.

"Kaitlyn!" Rebecca yelled, standing outside the car as she peered into the back seat through the window.

"Oh!" I yelped. Startled, I frantically began to gather my things.

"Fell asleep there, Kaitlyn?" Mr. Blaine joked.

"Just about," I replied with a smile. "Thanks so much for the ride, Mr. Blaine."

"Anytime, kid." He was always so kind, I thought to myself. I wondered how he could be anything but jovial behind closed doors. Perhaps I was about to find out. I scrambled out of the car, but to my surprise Rebecca hadn't even bothered to wait for me and was already halfway to the front door. A little shocked, I scurried to catch up.

"Hey, slow down," I said as I approached her.

"Took you long enough," she replied.

"Yeah, sorry. I completely zoned out during the ride over," I explained. The bitterness of her sour attitude was more noticeable now than it was in the car. What I struggled to understand was why she now directed her anger towards me. "So, what happened?"

"What do you mean?" she snapped.

"This morning, at your house. It seems like you're pissed about something."

Rebecca stopped dead in her tracks. "I'm not pissed – I'm sick. Didn't you hear me say that in the car?"

"Yeah, but it looks like more than just that," I replied, sheepishly. Rebecca looked as though she was on the verge of an outburst and I certainly didn't want to be the one to tip her over the edge.

She didn't answer. The remainder of our walk that morning was in silence. Rebecca marched a little faster than me, which gave me ample opportunity to analyze and dissect her facial expressions without notice. Eyes slightly squinted, I peered intensely in her direction. Rebecca had a fearful solemnness about her and illness certainly didn't fit the mark. I longed to have a conversation with her, to understand what it was that had caused this behavior, but my social interpretation of the situation made it clear that she hadn't the slightest interest in discussing the matter with me.

Rebecca and I had always been blatantly open with one another and so my arrival at such a conclusion was distressing. We shared our most embarrassing stories, our deepest secrets and the most awful truths about ourselves. But in this moment, it was as though we'd never done anything of the sort. It was as though a brick wall stood between us and will as I may to knock it down, it wouldn't budge. The uncertainty was killing me! And what made matters even worse was the fact that I never thought we'd keep *anything* from one another. Even the tiniest, most insignificant detail on a typical day would be communicated and talked to death – simply put, that's what we did, that's the way we were. Her behavior was completely uncharacteristic. What was it that irked her today, which prevented her from confiding in me the way she always had in the past? These were the questions to which I dreaded the answers.

Rebecca continued to storm ahead, racing down the stairs to the cafeteria. I continued after her, still hoping I'd be able to persuade her into some form of conversation before class. She quickly grabbed a muffin and paid the cashier. I wasn't but a moment behind her but before I could even open my mouth again she hastily stated, "I'm going to class early this morning to ask my teacher a few questions."

"Oh," I replied, a little surprised. Did she actually expect me to believe that? Reluctantly, I accepted her excuse and responded, "Okay, I guess I'll see you after school then."

"Sure," she answered, and quickly disappeared into the crowd.

Although I felt hurt by the fact that Rebecca had no intention of sharing her feelings with me, I did my best to dismiss the uncomfortable situation and respect her wishes. Convincing myself she'd tell me eventually, I unwrapped my muffin and broke off a piece as I walked to the middle of the caf where I spotted a few of my friends. Ellie, a fellow dancer, nodded my way from a table a little off to my left but before I could reach them, someone grabbed my right arm from behind.

"Kaitlyn!" It was Marcel, the one and only mutual friend Rebecca and I had at Leacrest. Without so much as a hello, Marcel quickly asked, "How's Rebecca today?" and he seemed nervous and jumpy.

Stunned by his question, I replied, "What do you mean?"

"You didn't hear?"

"Hear what?" I demanded as I felt my stomach jump.

"Chantel had her pinned against a locker yesterday – by her neck!" Marcel exclaimed.

"What?!" I yelled. My breath stopped, my body froze and my eyes grew wide. I felt my gaze slowly shift from Marcel, to the wall behind him and then to the floor where I watched my muffin fall. My muscles grew tense as I clenched my fists and slowly let my eyes meet Marcel's again. "Did you see it?" I don't know why I asked – I didn't want to know the answer. The horrible images racing through my mind were more than enough.

"Yes," answered Marcel, "it happened during third period."

I knew Marcel had a spare third period, as did Rebecca. Chantel? Who knew? Since the first day of school, I'd only seen her a handful of times in English and I had strategically chosen a new seat at the very front of the classroom so as to avoid close contact. It was obvious what kind of student she was, constantly skipping class, refraining from any form of participation when she did show up – and now this! Poor Rebecca, I thought to myself.

"How did this happen?" I questioned.

"Honestly, I don't really know," he said, shrugging his shoulders, "I was eating my lunch with a few buddies when I noticed a huge swarm of people form at those lockers over there," he said, pointing to the cove of lockers where, evidently, the incident had taken place. "I jumped out of my seat and began walking towards the crowd. I could hear a girl's voice and she was yelling. I climbed up the main stairs a few steps so I could get a better view when I saw it," he paused, seeming almost reluctant to continue and I could tell it was difficult for him to go on. Marcel had a big heart and if I didn't know any better, I'd say he'd developed a huge soft spot for Rebecca.

"Saw what?" I pressed.

"I couldn't see Rebecca's face, only Chantel's," he went on. "She was yelling and waving her hands all over the place."

"What was she saying?" I inquired, dying to know what had caused this terrible event.

"I couldn't make it out – the sounds of the crowd drowned out the words. But after a few seconds of Chantel yelling, I could tell her anger was mounting. Then she took her forearm, pinned it under Rebecca's chin and slammed her against the locker. Honestly, it was a pretty hard hit. The whole crowd gasped when it happened. Then it looked like Chantel whispered something in her ear. She gave Rebecca one last shove into her neck and then let her go and walked towards the crowd. But I could tell that Chantel had pinned her real hard because when she let her go I saw Rebecca fall forwards, coughing."

"Oh my," I said, my hand over my heart. I couldn't believe what I was hearing.

"I know. And after she let Rebecca go, Chantel faced the crowd and was almost taunting everyone, saying something like 'what are you looking at?' And within a few seconds everyone dispersed. *No one* went over to help Rebecca. I tried to run down the stairs but the crowd was so thick I couldn't get through and by the time I reached the bottom, she was nowhere to be found and I haven't seen her since."

"Oh no…" I trailed off. "No wonder…" I muttered under my breath.

"No wonder what?"

"Uh," I hesitated. "Nothing, nothing."

"Come on, Kaitlyn," Marcel said, sternly. "What? Tell me."

I looked into his eyes and could tell he was just as concerned as I. "She was just different this morning, that's all," I said vaguely, feeling guilty that I'd said anything at all.

"Different how?"

Reluctantly, I continued. "She was a little on edge…from the conversation that took place between her and her father in the car, it seemed as though something had occurred at her house that morning. It sounded as though Rebecca had told her parents she was sick and wanted to stay home but they insisted she come to school. I could tell she wasn't sick, though, and when we walked into school, I expected her to tell me what was really going on, but she didn't. I'm just so confused because we always tell each other everything."

"Kaitlyn, she probably didn't want to talk about it," said Marcel, trying his best to comfort me. "It's awful – and embarrassing," he added.

"Yeah, but it's *me*," I asserted.

"I know, but it's hard. She was literally assaulted by this stupid bully!" he exclaimed.

I despised that word. The stories I'd heard on the news from other schools disgusted me. I couldn't believe that now it was happening right here, right now, in our school. *And to my best friend.* It had to be stopped. How could Chantel get away with this? The troubling thought triggered my next series of questions.

"Were there no teachers around? What happened to Chantel after? Did no one report this?"

"I did."

"Oh, Marcel. That's so good of you. To who?"

"A guidance counselor. Mrs. Russo. She took down a bunch of notes as I told her the story," explained Marcel.

"I wonder what they'll do with her."

"I know, me too."

There was a moment of silence as I turned around to face the tainted lockers. As much as I could justify Rebecca's attempt to "play sick" and even her refusal to confide in me, the racing thoughts in my mind suddenly came to a head. And then it hit me. I had a serious issue on my hands. Now that I knew what had transpired the day prior, what was I to do with this information? Was I to confront Rebecca? Did she really think I'd never find out? In high school, word traveled faster than a speeding bullet. And if I informed her that I knew, should I tell her Marcel was the one who broke the news to me? She'd surely be embarrassed. I didn't want to upset her. And what about her parents? Was it my responsibility to tell them too? Rebecca would despise me for that. But what if matters got worse? I thought back to the incident that had taken place outside the cafeteria. Even though I was upset that this awful girl had been the storm cloud on what was supposed to be our perfect first day of school, the confrontation seemed fairly insignificant in hindsight. But now, it was quite the opposite. This occurrence marked the beginning of a horrifying sequence of events.

My mind raced on. It was the middle of October. This was the second of only two incidents I knew about since the start of school but I felt my heart fall into my stomach as I couldn't help but wonder – was this the second of two incidents, or was it the latest of several of which I was completely unaware? I pressed my mind to think back. I certainly noticed the barricade Rebecca had placed between us that morning, but tried to recollect whether or not I'd seen any indication that Chantel may have tormented her prior to yesterday. I'd certainly been preoccupied lately. Had I been too wrapped up in my own life to notice? The truth of the matter was, as I cast my thoughts back to days gone by, I realized that I hadn't paid much mind to the happenings around me. Had Rebecca acted differently before this morning? Certainly not to the extent of what I witnessed today, but maybe, just maybe I had missed something.

"Hey, you okay?" I heard Marcel's voice behind me.

"Oh – yeah," I said, shaking my head. "Sorry, I was trying to remember whether or not I'd seen Rebecca acting strangely on any other occasion over the last couple of months."

"Oh...why? Do you think that means something?" I could see the wheels in his head begin to spin.

"Well –" I hesitated, not wanting to state aloud what I now thought was an obvious fact, "Maybe this wasn't only the second time."

"The second time!?" Marcel exclaimed in shock. "What do you mean, second? This happened before?" His voice became almost shrill.

Again, I paused. I suppose the first encounter could hardly be considered an act of bullying. No! I stopped myself. This is exactly how students, teachers, parents – everyone who is a culprit of diminishing the severity of bullying – behave. Dismissing even the smallest of circumstances as unworthy of any real concern was a dangerous move. To me it was clear. Yesterday's escalated act was precipitated by the cafeteria confrontation. As insignificant as it seemed at the time, it was anything but. And I wasn't about to convince myself otherwise. But the truth was, I felt awful speaking about it to Marcel – almost embarrassed for Rebecca. Why did I feel embarrassed? It certainly wasn't her fault she'd somehow become the unfortunate target of a cruel game spawned by the insecurities of adolescence. There was no sensible reasoning behind it and so that's exactly what it felt like: an irrational, groundless – but dangerous – game. A game in which Chantel stood confidently in the dominant position while Rebecca wilted, slowly and sadly.

"Something happened on the first day of school," I muttered, reluctantly.

Marcel's eyes widened in shock.

"We didn't know you then," I explained, "and it wasn't anything nearly as awful as what happened yesterday," I went on, "but it upset me nonetheless. Actually, Rebecca didn't seem bothered by it in the slightest, but from my point of view, it tainted the entire first day of school." I sighed heavily as a wave of guilt rushed over me. Perhaps I shouldn't have been speaking to anyone about this until I'd had a chance to talk to Rebecca. Knee deep in my story, it was too late now. "Chantel confronted Rebecca outside the caf, claiming Rebecca had bumped into her from behind. I was standing with Rebecca at the time – if anything it was the slightest nudge," I explained. "It was ridiculous that Chantel said anything at all! She was clearly looking for a fight."

"Ugh," Marcel's expression was one of disgust, "poor Rebecca."

"I know. But the question is: what do we do now?"

"What *can* we do?" Marcel inquired. "I've already reported it. Now it's up to the school."

"We can't just wait around for the school to do something," I insisted. "What if they don't act on this? Or what if they just suspend her for a few days? That'll be useless! Chantel will return as if nothing happened, ready and willing to bully someone new or, what's more likely, Rebecca again!" My face grew hot and my palms began to sweat as I realized how little control we had over the situation.

Marcel leaned in and put his arm around me. As much as it felt good to be comforted, I couldn't help but think that the real person in need of comfort was Rebecca and yet she was the very person pushing away all those in her life capable of providing it.

Who did I think I was? What could I really do to help the situation? I planned to follow up with the guidance counselor Marcel had spoken to, but then what? I knew very well that whatever punishment the school gave Chantel – if any at all – likely wouldn't faze her. How could I take matters into my own hands? Chantel was intimidating. The very look in her eyes told you she was fearless, aggressive and capable of hateful acts others wouldn't dream of. What if I were to stand up to her? What would it take to get through to her? It seemed to me that the only way to have an impact on someone like Chantel was to communicate with her in a way she understood – on her level. Threats, physical violence, verbal abuse – this was the kind of approach to which Chantel might – just might – have a reaction. But how could I stoop to such a level? How I could I at once forget about my pride, my dignity and my demeanor. The likelihood of me, little old me, having even the slightest positive effect on the situation was slim to none. But there was a deeper truth at play here. A shameful fact. Plain and simple, I was afraid – afraid to be a target. I feared deeply that if I stood up to Chantel, her focus might make a fateful switch. I might become…her next victim.

6

I WISH I HADN'T

My palms were sweaty. My right leg shook nervously as I bobbed it up and down on the ball of my foot beneath the table. I gazed down at my phone every few seconds to check the time. She was three minutes late. I had arrived early – nerves I suppose. I cupped my hands around the latte I purchased just a few moments ago, blowing gently through the hole in the lid to cool it down. I was desperate to take a sip – more than anything else I think I merely needed something to do to pass the time other than stare at my phone. Mirroring that morning's events, Rebecca had been excessively quiet and unwilling to speak on the way home from school. I suppose I couldn't blame her and I was grateful that she'd agreed to meet for coffee that evening. "Our Spot" (at least that's how we referred to the coffee shop around the corner from our homes) was where we always met if we were in need of a private one-on-one. Usually, we'd walk over together but I decided to make Our Spot the venue for my homework completion that night and so I instructed Rebecca to meet me there at 9:00pm. Although at first reluctant, I managed to convince her. As I stared down at my piping hot coffee, I heard the bells chime on the door as it slowly opened. The cool night breeze made me shudder in my seat. She'd arrived.

"Hi," I waved.

She walked towards me, a very slight but welcoming smile on her face. I instantly felt relieved. Small as it was, the little grin was the first pleasant expression I'd seen from Rebecca all day. She slung her purse strap over the left corner of the chair opposite me, pulled her scarf and let it slowly unravel from her neck, and then slowly inched her way out of the beige fall coat that hugged her body so snuggly. And then I saw it. A small, yet unmistakable mark on her neck. My body froze. I knew what Chantel had done, but I didn't think the results of her actions would have left any noticeable injury. But there it was: a purplish-blue smudge on the left side of her neck – the remnant of a terrible event.

My face must have said it all because as my eyes shifted upwards from Rebecca's neck, she looked alarmed. "What's wrong?" she inquired, slinking down into her seat.

Was she actually making an attempt to deny why I'd called her here? Did she think I hadn't heard? "Your –" I couldn't get my words out. "Your neck..." I trailed off.

Rebecca turned white as a ghost. Her lips slowly separated as she searched to find the right words and the ones she chose took me by surprise. "What do you mean?" she asked innocently, her right hand coming up to feel her neck.

"The bruise, Rebecca," I answered in an assertive tone I was most certain she'd construe as that coming from a person who knew exactly what had happened.

"What?" She exclaimed, sounding genuinely shocked. Her right hand cupped around her neck, Rebecca jumped from her seat and headed towards what I could only assume was the bathroom.

Seriously? I thought to myself. How could she possibly be unaware of the bruise? And if she did in fact know it was there and I pointed it out, why on Earth was she still trying to hide this from me? Had our relationship deteriorated *that* much over the past couple of months? Had we drifted so far apart that she could no longer confide in me? Whatever her approach to the situation, I firmly solidified my position: I wasn't backing down.

After what seemed like eternity, I felt Rebecca brush by my right shoulder and slowly slouch back down into her seat. Her head hung low as if the very life had been sucked out of her. She let her elbows hit down heavily onto the table as her head fell into her hands. I heard a quiet sob from my seat on the other side of the table and I reached out to touch her arm.

"Ugh," she said as she looked up at me. Her eyes red and swollen, her face wet with fresh tears, to my surprise she let out a small chuckle.

I smiled. "It's okay."

"I didn't notice the bruise before…" she said, ever so quietly.

"Sometimes it takes a while for them to show," I replied.

Rebecca shook her head and I could tell she was trying hard not to cry.

"It's okay," I repeated.

We sat in silence for a few moments. Understanding she needed time but eager to hear her side of the story, I prodded softly, "Can you tell me what happened?"

"Oh, Kaitlyn," she sobbed. "I can't tell you how much I just don't want to talk about it."

"I know it's hard, Rebecca, but I'm here to help you," I insisted.

Her sadness instantly turned to anger, "Help me?" she remarked in disbelief. "Help me?" she repeated, louder this time, "how the hell are *you* going to help *me*?"

Confused by her sudden change in disposition, I went on to explain myself, "Well, you can talk it out with me. Maybe I can make you feel better about the situation and hopefully, together, we can come up with a solution to put an end to it."

She laughed sarcastically. "Are you kidding me?"

"What do you mean?" I asked, quite puzzled by her facetious response.

As unprepared as I was for her behavior until now, I was equally shocked for what came next. "Kaitlyn, let me tell you something. You have absolutely no idea what I'm going through. What happened at school yesterday – I don't even want to think about it, not even for a minute. It's been the only thing on my mind ever since. I'm painfully embarrassed and I can't even bear the thought of what other students must think of me…"

"Rebecca, that's –" But she wouldn't let me finish.

"No don't," she said, holding up her hand, "it's horrifying. I don't even know how I made it to school today. I tried so hard to play the sick card with my parents but they knew I wasn't. I just *couldn't* see her today, you know? Thank goodness I didn't. I don't know what I did to this girl, but she has it in for me."

"How did this happen?" I persisted.

"I didn't do anything, if that's what you're getting at," Rebecca answered defensively.

"I'm not saying that," I assured her.

"Honestly, I was just walking by and unfortunately we made eye contact," I could see the tears begin to stream down her face. "And that was it. She then went off and screamed at me, 'What are you looking at?' I didn't even answer her, I just tried to keep walking but she grabbed my arm and spun me around to face her, put her arm against my neck and slammed me against the lockers, screaming, 'I *said*, what are you looking at?' I had no idea what to say…" Now Rebecca was crying even harder. "She just kept shoving me deeper and deeper into the lockers as if she was trying to push me right through. She used so much force on my neck that it was actually hard to breathe. No wonder I have a bruise now…"

"Oh, Rebecca!" It broke my heart – hearing her account of the incident as I tried, somehow, to understand what she was going through. But I knew I couldn't – and she did too. The hurt, the frustration, the humiliation – it was overwhelming even to *think* about, let alone experience. Relieved she told me, but afraid only the wrong words would come out of my mouth, I stayed silent. I wanted to cry too, but I knew it was best to stay strong. After a few minutes, I said sternly, "When do you want to tell your parents?"

Rebecca's eyes widened. "No way," she responded firmly, "Kaitlyn, I'm serious. No matter what, you cannot tell them."

"What!?" I couldn't believe what I was hearing. "Why?"

Her tone was now condescending and offensive. "You really don't get it do you?" I felt my cheeks turn crimson red.

"If I tell my parents, they'll march into that school, talk to the principal, and embarrass the hell out of me! I don't need to solve this – I need to forget it ever happened. What do you think they'll honestly do to Chantel? Give her detention? Suspend her? They're not going to expel her…not a single teacher saw what happened! She'll find out my parents did this and come after me even harder. Is that what you want?"

"Obviously not, Rebecca, but we have to do something!"

"Kaitlyn, let it go. This is something that needs to pass naturally. I'm just her target right now. If we just leave it alone, she'll find someone new. But I'm begging you, if you're really my best friend you'll stay quiet. You can't tell anyone. I mean no one! You have no idea what this is like and it's not your business to fix it."

"But I want to tell our parents *because* you're my best friend!" I exclaimed. "You just want me to sit back and do nothing? I can't. It's not right. Marcel saw what happened yesterday, you know, and he filed a report with one of the guidance counselors." (Turns out this only amounted to a 'serious talk' with Chantel since no one of authority saw what happened.)

"No, he didn't," Rebecca said, mounting frustration in her voice. "I can't believe this," she added, jumping up from her seat and grabbing her coat. "This is *my* business and *my* problem – not yours and Marcel's!" With that, she stomped assertively towards the door and disappeared into the dark night.

I scrambled to grab whatever things I had with me and quickly ran out after her. But I was already too late. Rebecca's brisk walk had turned to a sprint and I saw her running far ahead of me towards our street. "Rebecca!" I screamed.

She was long gone.

7

THE DILEMMA

My eyes were open but all I could see was the pitch-black darkness of night. I lay there in my bed, hands clasped tightly over my chest and comforter pulled right up to my chin. Heart palpitating faster than usual and stomach churning uneasily down below, I replayed the evening's events in my mind.

Although I'd been nervous to confront Rebecca, I was entirely unprepared for what had happened…her resistance to my help, her refusal to tell our parents and the way she so despairingly pleaded with me to keep quiet. As much as I hated to admit it, I felt resentful towards her. I thought it to be entirely unfair of her to expect me to continue on with my life nonchalantly as if I knew nothing. Did she not understand how much she meant to me? Her emotions were clear proof of how gravely upset she was about what had transpired and yet her unreasonable, senseless requests alluded to the idea that this was no big deal! How could she possibly believe everything would just disappear?

Even if Chantel chose a new victim as the primary recipient of her malicious actions, it was entirely unjust for us to sit back and let her walk away without due punishment. Not only was it right for her to pay the price for what she did to Rebecca, but we also had a moral responsibility to the next person, did we not? Who knows how many people she'd already bullied? If we did nothing, the cycle would only continue. More people would be hurt and Chantel wouldn't have the slightest inclination to change because she'd never suffered any consequences as a result of her actions.

I let out a heavy sigh and turned onto my right side, sliding my arm beneath the pillow. My mind shifted back to Rebecca – happy, kind and energetic Rebecca. At least that's the friend I'd known for the last thirteen years. But she's not the girl who came to the coffee shop that night. The girl who walked through those doors just a few hours earlier had a certain graveness about her. She appeared somber and subdued and her eyes were tired. Her warming smile and lively spirit were nowhere to be seen. I noticed her shoulders hung low as she slouched in her chair, sinking deep into its wooden frame. I imagine she looked exactly as she felt…damaged. I could feel her heavy heart from where I sat.

Although I was grateful for the fact that Rebecca had opened up to me at least a little, it wasn't enough. I was profoundly worried about her and I feared that over time, matters would only worsen. Our conversation was so brief that I didn't even have a chance to ask her if there had been other incidents between her and Chantel. Even without an answer, my instincts told me there were – and if I was right, this would only further prove my prediction that another encounter was just around the corner. And yet here I lay, still in my bed – a silenced friend. From my perspective, I wasn't a friend at all…far from it, in fact. A real friend would have told someone, spoken out, taken action in some way. But I didn't. As much as I felt the opposing, contradictory pulls of my dilemma deep inside, I was far too afraid to disobey Rebecca's wishes. She'd confided in me that night. Even though it was only for a few minutes and despite the fact that it ended badly, there was still meaning in it. Didn't Rebecca need a friend more than anything else right now? If I turned against her, all trust would be lost. She'd dismiss me the same way she had earlier that morning.

As my mind's whirlwind of thoughts began to spiral in the opposite direction, I felt my eyes grow heavy and tired. I blinked once and then slowly reopened my eyes to the darkness around me. No, I told myself, keeping quiet was the best way. How could I betray my best friend? How could I even contemplate going against her wishes after everything she'd been through? And who knows, perhaps Rebecca was right. These kinds of incidents happen all the time. Kids get over it and bullies grow up. I wasn't the one on the other end of the attacks. How could I possibly understand what she was going through and how she felt? Who was I to decide what was best? I'd believed in Rebecca all my life. Why was I second-guessing her judgment now? Just as she said, it was her life and her business. It was my duty to respect her wishes. At the right time, I'd talk to her again and maybe – eventually – I'd be able to change her mind.

The hallway was long. Dim light fixtures hung between the doors of each apartment. The one closest to me dangled loosely from the wall, its wires exposed. A deep, maroon-colored floral paper covered the walls, its corners peeling back at the seams. It smelled of stale clothing – a scent that reminded me of the armoire in our spare bedroom where Mom stored extra blankets, sheets and tablecloths. There was no time to think – the alarm sounded, piercingly and almost unbearably loud. Crisp and clear, it rang through my ears. I wanted desperately to cover them but I needed my arms to run. Ever so faintly I could make out the red EXIT sign at the very far end of the hallway. I began to race towards it but my legs were so heavy I could barely lift them. Every stride was a struggle. As I slowly passed the apartment doors on either side of me, I began to smell smoke. Still I ran, my eyes glued to the faintly illuminated red letters straight ahead. But the more ground I covered, the thicker the smoke became and the less I could see. My eyes burned and I began to pant as I continued my attempts to run further and further down the hallway. After a while I ran blindly, smoke clouding my vision. I stopped and leaned forward, my hands on my knees as I heaved huge breaths in and out. When I opened my eyes, I realized I could no longer see the floor through the thick cloud of smoke that consumed me. I began to cough uncontrollably. My eyes watered and my chest ached. Beep…beep…beep… The alarm was all I could hear.

I gasped for air. Breathing deeply with my hand over my chest, I attempted to catch my breath. Beep…beep…beep… I reached over and slammed the "off" button on the clock atop my night table. My body was covered in a thin layer of sweat. As my breath slowly returned to normal, I began to wipe the beads of perspiration from my forehead.

"Are you alright?" Mom's voice sounded from my doorway.

Feeling totally discombobulated, I replied, "Oh, yeah…I just had an awful dream."

As Mom walked closer, her eyes widened. "Wow, I can see that," she said. "Do you want to talk about it?"

"Um…" I hesitated. Normally I would have, but I felt flustered and didn't want to be late for the Blaines again. "You know what, Mom, not now. But thanks."

"You sure?" she confirmed, looking into my eyes. "You don't look so good."

"Yeah, I didn't get much sleep last night."

"Why not? Is there something on your mind?" she asked. Moms always know, don't they?

Oh, how I so desperately wanted to tell her. How easy it would be to let it all out. To accept her love and comfort. To instantly feel better.

"No, no, I'm okay," I lied.

"Okay, well let me know if you change your mind and want to talk. I'm around tonight," she told me.

"I will. Thanks, Mom."

I was nearly in the clear but then she paused mid-step on her way out the door and asked, "How was the coffee shop last night? Did you and Rebecca have fun?"

My heart jumped into my throat. Mom and I had such an open, honest relationship. I felt terrible lying to her but Rebecca's words raced through my mind. "Yeah, we did," I said, forcing my most genuine, phony smile.

"Good," Mom replied, slapping her hand definitively against my bedroom doorframe as she walked out.

I threw the covers off and stepped out of bed. Well, that settled it. If there was anybody I would have broken my promise for it was Mom – and I didn't. As I thought about the troubling circumstance one last time, I decided that all in all, it was more important for Rebecca to stay in communication with me so I could be there to help her in whatever way she needed. There would be no telling of what happened. Not to Mom, not to Dad, not to Jacob. Although I was always one to doubt my decisions, in that moment I remembered the quote from Shakespeare's King Lear that Dad had recited on so many an occasion:

"No, I will weep no more. In such a night

To shut me out? Pour on; I will endure.

In such a night as this? O Regan, Goneril!

Your old kind father, whose frank heart gave all—

O, that way madness lies; let me shun that;

No more of that."

And with that, I agreed: "that way, madness lies". My silence was affirmed.

8

LIFE AFTER

I assumed my regular seat in the back of Mr. Blaine's car. Everyday his routine was the same: about 10 minutes before our scheduled departure time, Mr. Blaine would pull the car out of the garage and leave it running in the driveway to warm up as he gathered his things. Today, I was the first one in.

"Good morning," I said cheerily as Mr. Blaine and Rebecca entered the car.

"Morning Kaitlyn," Mr. Blaine's voice was louder than Rebecca's but I could hear her faint greeting in the background. I felt relieved she'd responded at all and prayed today's morning wouldn't mirror that of yesterday. Our ride to school made me feel as though everything had been restored to its natural state. Mr. Blaine cursed at the bad drivers on the road and cracked sarcastic jokes that made me chuckle from the backseat. I peered through the reflection in the passenger side mirror to see Rebecca's smile as she rolled her eyes at him. We casually discussed the day's events and told Mr. Blaine about our most loved and hated teachers at school. He spoke of the dreaded tasks to be completed at work and how he wished he were retired. For a few moments, I forgot about last night. It was nice. Upon our arrival, we bid our farewells to Mr. Blaine, grabbed our bags and made our way towards the school.

"So –" Rebecca and I chimed in simultaneously. Then we chuckled awkwardly.

"You first," I insisted.

"Well," she began awkwardly, "I just wanted to say that I'm sorry for the way I acted last night. I'm just such a mess over this whole situation."

"I know," I replied, "And I'm sorry too. I don't mean to be pushy or forceful. I'm just worried and I want to be here for you. It just kills me when you block me out – like you did yesterday morning…"

"Yeah…" her voice trailed off, "it's just embarrassing. When I talk about it, I'm reminded of what happened, and truthfully, it's something I'm trying desperately to forget."

"I can imagine."

As we continued our usual morning walk through the front doors of the school and down the main flight of stairs to the foyer, I smiled to myself. My best friend was back. Despite my doubts and reservations about our bully's intentions to prevent a repetition of her behavior, I felt a sense of relief. The connection between us had been at least partially restored and it had me convinced our troubles were over. I so genuinely wanted to believe Rebecca was right – that in time, it would all just disappear.

We walked into the cafeteria to enjoy our usual breakfast of champions – those delicious, freshly baked muffins. Today I splurged for a chocolate chip and Rebecca chose blueberry. As we waited in line at the cash register, I spotted Marcel outside the cafeteria. "Oh, there's Marcel," I pointed out.

She peered outside the door, smiled and waved at him. Her cheeks flushed a pinkish hue. As I stood and watched her, I was more confident than ever that she most certainly had feelings for him. As I switched my gaze back to Marcel, my supposition was only further confirmed by his huge, genuine and infectious smile. They'd make a terrific couple, I thought to myself. And then it dawned on me – today was Friday! Without any concrete social plans in place, I decided to propose a get together that night. I'd likely feel like a third wheel in the scenario, but right now, Rebecca's happiness was of the greatest importance and I felt compelled to play matchmaker. An evening out would be just the thing Rebecca needed to take her mind off Chantel.

Muffins paid for, we made our way out the cafeteria door. "Hi, Marcel," I greeted him as I unraveled the wrap around my muffin.

"Hey guys, how are you?" Marcel answered (looking only at Rebecca).

"Good," Rebecca answered, eyes glowing and cheeks flush. As her left hand reached up towards her neck, I couldn't help but notice how tightly she'd wound her scarf. I assumed the hand gesture was a way to ensure it was still covering her unsightly bruise. I wondered it if looked worse today than it had last night.

"Listen, a buddy of mine is having a few people over tonight. Actually, Kaitlyn, Jacob and his buddies will be there too. Thought maybe you two might want to come," Marcel said.

Perfect! This way I wouldn't be a third wheel and these two would have a chance to spend some time together. "That sounds like fun!" I replied, enthusiastically.

"Yeah, sure," Rebecca agreed.

"Great, I'll let him know. He probably lives about ten minutes from you two, think you'll be able to get a ride?"

"I'm sure my mom will drive us," I replied.

"Great!" Marcel seemed genuinely excited. "I'll text you his address later today. Come around 7:00pm."

"Okay!" Rebecca and I answered in unison.

"Alright, well, I have to run to class a little early today but I'll see you both later," Marcel gave us a little wave as he walked away.

Rebecca and I looked at one another and smiled. We were in for a fun night.

"**H**ave a great time, girls, and be safe," Mom grinned. She looked just as excited as we were. *Be safe*, I repeated the phrase in my mind. No matter what the occasion, these were always Mom's last words to me whenever I left the house.

"We will," I assured her, "thanks so much for the ride, Mom.

"No problem. Midnight pickup, right?"

"If you must," I answered, sarcastically. Over the last few months, as I began to make new friends, I felt entitled to a later curfew. 1:00am would have been nice, but I knew it was a long shot tonight. We were only in the second month of high school and I'd already persuaded my parents to extend the time from 11:30pm to 12:00am. This would have to do for now.

"Thank you, Mrs. Lee," Rebecca chimed in, "midnight is perfect."

"See you then!" Mom waved goodbye through the window.

As we turned around and walked towards the house, I eagerly grabbed hold of Rebecca's arm and said, "So…are you excited?"

"Actually, I am," she answered funnily. "And you know…" her voice trailed off a little.

"What?" I asked. Her tone had piqued my curiosity.

She paused and stared straight ahead. There it was, that blush again! And then she spoke shyly, "I think I like Marcel."

"Ahhh!" I let out a shriek of excitement. "I knew it!"

"Really?" she asked, doubtfully.

"Are you kidding me? Yes. Annnd…" I said sneakily.

"And what?"

"And…I'm pretty sure Marcel likes you too," I told her.

"Seriously?"

"Seriously."

Her cheeks turned crimson red. In that moment, I felt genuinely delighted for her. I realized nothing had come to fruition just yet but I'll never forget how happy she looked that night. The elated emotions of a first crush, the excitement of the unknown, the playful flirtations that were sure to come – I couldn't wait for her to experience every moment.

Rebecca rang the doorbell and a few seconds later a handsome blonde answered the door. He had a smile that instantly put you at ease and a mesmerizing set of jet blue eyes.

"Hey!" he exclaimed.

"Hi," I reached out my hand to shake his. "I'm Kaitlyn and this is Rebecca. Thanks so much for having us."

"You bet! Come on in," he stepped to the side, opened the door a little wider and ushered us into the main foyer, "I'm Sebastian."

I liked that name. "Nice to meet you," I answered.

"Hey!" I heard Marcel's voice holler from inside the house. "You girls made it. C'mon over here!"

We followed the boys into the family room where some guests stood in groups chatting and laughing and others sat on the couches watching the hockey game.

"Do you gals want a beer or a cooler?"

Before I could answer for myself, Rebecca chimed in, "We'll have two coolers, please. Thanks!"

I quickly voiced my agreement, "Yeah, that sounds great."

"Two coolers coming right up," Sebastian walked out of the family room and into the kitchen.

While he was gone, Marcel took the liberty of introducing us to the rest of the people at the party and it didn't take long for me to find Jacob. Sebastian was back with our drinks in no time and from that point forward, the party seemed to take us over in a whirl of excitement. Drinks in hand and permanent smiles painted on our faces, Rebecca and I were having a blast. Jacob and I quickly fell into our groove but the magic didn't last long…

As the time ticked by, I could feel the alcohol setting in. All too aware of the mental and physical changes I was feeling, I set my drink down on the table next to me. Given her fragile state, I felt it was my duty to keep an eye on Rebecca. Every time I took a second to peer over at her, she was talking, smiling and laughing with Marcel – until the last time my eyes turned in her direction. My brow furrowed as I struggled to pinpoint what looked different all of a sudden, and then it hit me – her neck! Her scarf now hung loosely below the nape of her neck, exposing her awful bruise. My heart sank to the floor. I had to cover her up! But Jacob was knee deep in a story and I didn't want to be rude. Forget it, she meant far more to me than him.

I quickly told him I needed a second and walked briskly towards Rebecca and Marcel. But it was too late. As I walked closer, I could hear Marcel faintly say the words, "…she did this to you?" Rebecca looked horrified as she clasped her left hand over her neck and noticed the scarf was missing. Then it was like a game of dominos as one after another, people's heads turned to face the two of them. I could hear the whispers all around us, "What?" … "*She's* the girl?" … "Is that her?" … "The one Chantel had against the locker?" I grabbed Rebecca's arm for support. She looked at me in disbelief. Now the whispers became yells as people directed their questions directly at Rebecca, loud enough for everyone to hear. "Chantel pinned you against the locker?" … "What did you do to her?" … "She gave you that mark on your neck?" … "Are you okay?"

Only a few moments had passed but it felt like eternity. It was clear that Rebecca hadn't the faintest idea how to answer or how to act. The partygoers weren't cruel or insensitive to the circumstance – just curious. Everyone wanted to know if Rebecca was, in fact, the bully victim. But it was too much for her. She grabbed my hand and rushed us both out of the party. As we quickly made our way to the door, I could hear Marcel and Jacob bellowing after us. Rebecca slammed the door and walked directly to the curb. She plunked herself down and I sat next to her, embracing her tightly as she began to sob.

"Rebecca, are you okay?" Marcel asked as he knelt down in front of us.

Without moving she responded, "I'll be fine." Her voice was muffled, as her head hung down low between her knees.

I gave him a sympathetic look.

"I'm so sorry I even brought it up – it just shocked me, that's all," he desperately tried to explain himself and his face told me how badly he felt for causing such a commotion. "I was worried."

"It's okay," she answered, still not looking up. "It's not your fault." Rebecca lifted her head and stared straight ahead. "It was nice to forget for a while, you know?"

Marcel placed his hands on her knees and answered, "I know. It's over now, though. Please come back into the party."

"I can't," Rebecca answered, "I'm so embarrassed.

"Okay, I understand," Marcel was so great with her. "I'll wait with you until your ride comes."

Jacob tried to join us at the curb, but I ushered him away knowing perfectly well that the last thing Rebecca needed right now was a crowd around her. I reached in my pocket and checked my phone. It was only 11:00pm. "I'll call my Mom and ask her to come get us now."

"No!" Rebecca exclaimed. "Not yet…she can't see me crying."

"Really?" I asked in disbelief.

"Kaitlyn, please," Rebecca looked at me sternly. No more words were spoken but I could read the thoughts that circled through her mind. I had vowed to keep her incident a secret and tonight, she expected me to keep it.

"Okay," I answered calmly.

Marcel moved to sit on Rebecca's left and I stayed on her right. For the majority of the hour we spent on that curb waiting for our ride, we remained silent. Eventually, Rebecca stopped crying and the most recent events of the evening seemed to slowly drift away. Before long, we composed ourselves and gratefully hopped into Mom's car at midnight.

9

ROMEO AND JULIET

" 'See how she leans her cheek upon her hand! O that I were a glove upon that hand, that I might touch that cheek!' " Mr. Kemp recited from one of the world's greatest plays, Romeo and Juliet. His voice was spellbinding and he had my undivided attention. There's something special about watching a person immersed in their passion.

Be it literature, dance, music, construction, architecture – the feeling is always the same. When people do what they love, it oozes through every cell in their body and clear for all to see. Through facial expressions and body language, the passion is palpable. They are true masters at work. This was Mr. Kemp – a lover of English literature. The way he pronounced the words, how the tone of his voice changed to emphasize a particular phrase, and the emotion he portrayed as he read aloud…it was as though he were an actor in a play, not a teacher in a classroom. I found it incredibly inspiring and I listened intently as he continued to read from Act II, Scene II. As a result of Mr. Kemp's poignant recitation skills, I could feel the entire class slip a little deeper into the play, when suddenly the door opened.

I turned my head to see who it was and instantly snapped out of my trance. There she stood – tangled hair, shirt fallen off one shoulder and her jeans shoved messily into her boots. Chantel. As she trudged disruptively into the room, she flashed me an icy stare before walking down one of the rows to claim her seat at the back. Despite the fact that her entrance was such a blatantly rude interruption to the reading, Mr. Kemp ignored her and continued on without so much as a pause. Behind me I could hear her sit down, plunk her bag loudly onto the floor until at last, the room was restored to its quiet state. She hadn't attended class for at least three weeks – long before the locker incident with Rebecca. Realizing I hadn't heard anything, I wondered if she'd been suspended. The very sight of her made my blood boil.

Oh, how I wanted to stand up and scream at the top of my lungs, to tell the whole class what she'd done. I sat there, heart beating quickly, wishing Mr. Kemp knew. I wanted to hurt her...yank her long, tangled, fake-colored hair, punch her attitude-ridden face, and knee her right in the stomach. Wasn't it only fair that she feel pain too? I slowly and sneakily peered over my left shoulder to catch a quick glimpse of her snapping her gum, staring out the window unengaged, her arms crossed and her body slouched down low in her chair. What an ugly sight, I thought to myself. As much as I wanted to do something – anything – I knew I couldn't. I thought of Rebecca and unwillingly minded my own business.

Over the next few months our lives were restored to a more normal state. Within a week, Rebecca's bruise healed and after the night of the party, we didn't speak of what happened ever again. I knew the only way Rebecca would be able to fully move on, was if she weren't constantly reminded of past encounters. I still wondered if there had been more than the two I knew of, but didn't dare ask.

Marcel and Rebecca grew closer – very close in fact. Just a few weeks after the party, they became "official". I couldn't have been happier and I thought them to be a terrific match. Seeing how intimate their relationship had become, I never questioned why Rebecca and I had begun to spend less time together. I merely assumed that the majority of her free time was spent with him – and of course, mine with Jacob. Even though on most days Rebecca and I still traveled to and from school together and shared an evening coffee at our local spot here and there, our relationship wasn't what it was.

At times I resented Marcel for it often felt as though he'd stolen my best friend from right underneath me, but those thoughts were quickly dismissed and replaced by reminders of how happy Rebecca was. A girl who'd been through such abusive and traumatic incidents in months passed, who was I to burst her bubble? It's funny, you know. I used to regret feeling the way I did – missing my friend and wishing Marcel hadn't entered her life, and yet now, my regrets are the quite the opposite. I regret the fact that I never *acted* on those thoughts. I should have looked closer, pried deeper, followed my instincts. But how could I have known? Hindsight is 20/20. There were moments when I longed to reach out, talk to her, ask her to spend more time with me, inquire about her life, make sure everything was okay – but I always stopped myself. I feared I would be nothing more than a bother to her, a nagging friend who couldn't accept the fact that she'd met her first love. I remember constantly reassuring myself, convincing myself that she was fine because she had Marcel.

It was the middle of March when I really began to take notice of Rebecca's strange behavior. She became very private and introverted. When

I tried to talk to her on the way home from school, she gave short, abrupt answers. Not wanting to pry or force conversation, I remained quiet.

A few times I asked if she was alright and she quickly responded, "Yes, why?" Her answers were cold and hasty. I can't count the number of times I asked her to coffee but she always refused, saying she had somewhere else she had to be. Sometimes it was plans with Marcel, other times a family get-together and sometimes even an extra music lesson. It wasn't long before I felt as though I'd lost her as a friend entirely. I often thought of speaking to Marcel about it, partly because I wanted to make sure she was okay and partly because I had hopes that perhaps he would give up some of his time to make room for me. But I never did. I didn't feel comfortable talking to Marcel about Rebecca – I felt as though it would have been some kind of betrayal. The two of them were so close. I didn't want to intrude or interrupt what had so clearly become real love. How could I impede on Rebecca's happiness?

My diluted frame of mind began the night at the coffee shop. I had become so preoccupied with Rebecca's happiness, with my unwavering commitment to abide by her rules, that my vision was clouded. Was I right or wrong? Trustworthy or foolish? A friend or an accomplice?

What I wouldn't give to have that time back, to have the opportunity to do what felt right, to speak to others, to tell people everything I knew. Even if it didn't amount to anything, at least it would have been easier to live with myself. At least I wouldn't be haunted by a guilt and regret so strong that at one point it was difficult even to see my own reflection in the mirror. I didn't know who I was or where I was going. The single fact that stood tried and true in my mind was that I was someone who not only let down her friend but herself too. Each day was impossible to bear and yet there was nothing I could do to change it. If I'd spoken my thoughts, if I'd made a move, would it still have happened? On that brisk, sunny spring day, would we still have lost her?

10

THE BEGINNING
OF THE END

Iblinked twice hard. Tears fell from my eyes and landed on the tousled patch of grass below me. I gasped for air as I fell to my knees. Placing my hand on the earth, I scoured the area as if to find the answers, to discover some form of explanation for what I'd just witnessed. Spots of blood sprinkled the patch of grass where the brutal beating had taken place. How I wanted to see her, to hold her, to tell her she'd be okay. But I couldn't. My body felt as though it weighed a thousand pounds. I don't know how long I knelt there crying, but in those moments, the world stood still. Time didn't exist. Oh, but it did. Little did I know that what happened every second I knelt there uselessly on the field, was critical.

Finally, I managed to peel myself off the ground, eyes so puffy and swollen I could barely see. As I stood up straight and raised my eyes, I noticed a crowd of people surrounding me, staring. How long had they been there? I turned my head from left to right, scanning the mass. There must have been at least a hundred people there. I began to walk towards the school and the circle parted to let me through. Just a few steps later, I began to realize how important it was that I find Rebecca. My walk turned to a run as I made my way towards the school to find the one teacher I knew who rushed the field: Mr. Kemp. Barging through the doors, I raced through the cafeteria and up the stairs towards the office.

I slammed through the office doors and yelled, "Where's Mr. Kemp?"

The teachers and guidance counselors who were huddled around the main reception desk instantly looked up at me, bewildered expressions on their faces. At first no one answered.

My heart beat faster. "Where is he!?" I demanded, feeling myself lose control by the second.

Mrs. Lauder, one of the school's receptionists, answered, "He had to leave for the day. Is there something I can help you with?"

"Where did he go? I saw him helping the girl outside–" I gasped for air between my words and disjointed thought processes. "Where is he? Is he with her? Does he know what hospital they took her to?"

They stared, unsure of what to say and how much information to give.

"Umm...do you know her?" One woman asked.

"Yes!" my voice was shrill. "Yes, I do. She's my best friend...please someone help me..."

"Oh dear, I'm so sorry. We do not have any details to give you."

"Are you serious?!" I yelled. "I need to know where she is! I have to get there."

The more I talked, the more hysterical I sounded. These people didn't know me. As the minutes went by, I looked like less and less of the type of person they should be providing with private information. I wanted to scream at the top of my lungs in frustration.

I stared back at them, panting and sobbing. "Thanks for nothing," I finally said and walked away.

It was time to think logically. I took a deep breath. What was the closest hospital I knew of? North Lake. Go! I ordered an Uber. My stomach churned with fresh nerves, knowing very well my parents would be angry because I wasn't permitted to take Ubers on my own. But there was no time for public transit. I had to move fast.

True to form, the Uber came in a couple of minutes. I knew the hospital was only about five minutes from our high school but it felt as though we were in the car for hours. How badly I wanted to know if Rebecca was okay – if she was awake, unconscious, badly injured. My mind flooded with images of the gruesome attack. I grimaced in the back seat and turned my head towards the window to hide my emotions, but it was impossible. The Uber driver must have known something was wrong. I didn't care. As soon as the car pulled up, I muttered a fast thank you, scurried out and ran inside the ER. Whipping my head left to right, I frantically searched for familiar faces in the waiting area.

"Kaitlyn!" I heard Mr. Kemp's booming voice in the far left corner and I began to walk hastily towards him. "What are you doing here?" he asked, nervously. As I stared in shock, I couldn't believe the sight of him. He stood there disheveled in his blood-stained blazer and khakis, his body faintly trembling beneath the clothes. I was surprised he could even get a word out, but then he shakily made another inquiry, "How did you know?"

While Mr. Kemp certainly had no idea that I'd witnessed the painful episode, he was aware of our friendship. He'd been privy to the strength of our relationship since the high school held its Holiday Dance in December. A volunteer chaperone that evening, Mr. Kemp had greeted Rebecca and I at the door as we walked in. Even though he taught each of us English in separate periods, prior to that night's dance event he didn't know we were friends. We shared a casual and humorous conversation as he took a keen interest in the history of our friendship. Since that day, Rebecca and I spoke highly of Mr. Kemp, always referring to him as our favorite teacher.

I bypassed his questions and abruptly demanded, "Where is she?"

"With the doctors," he managed to mutter.

"What did they say?" I stammered on, focusing only on my best friend regardless of the fact that it was impossible to ignore Mr. Kemp's state. Here was a man who clearly needed help of his own.

"Nothing yet," he responded, "but the good news is that they took her in as soon as we got here in the ambulance." Mr. Kemp paused and then asked again, "How did you know to come here?"

"Took a guess," I told him.

"Oh," he seemed stunned and confused. He paused for a long while, staring into the hospital's triage waiting area, a look of utter despair on his face. What did he know that I didn't? How did Rebecca look and feel when he ran to her on the field? What happened before the firetruck arrived? All I could do was stare at him. After what seemed like an eternity, he covered his mouth with his hands and two tears streamed down each cheek.

I didn't know what to do. Or say. The state of my teacher – my usually strong, confident, happy and composed teacher – made me even more worried than I already was. That's when a new sensation came over my body and I knew I had to run, "I'm gonna be sick!"

I ran to the closest garbage can I could find, knowing I'd never make it to the washroom. Feeling the stares of the triage inhabitants burning through my back, I stayed hunched over not sure what to do next. Embarrassed, disgusted and not caring nearly enough to let it keep me from getting more answers, I forced myself to walk back to Mr. Kemp.

"Are her parents on their way?" I inquired.

"Kaitlyn, are you okay?" Mr. Kemp asked, concern in his voice.

"Forget it," I said. "Are her parents on their way?" I asked again.

"I told the office staff to phone her parents immediately, so yes, I believe so."

"What kind of state was she in?" The words dribbled out of my mouth – the most dreaded question of all. My stomach churned with debilitating anxiety.

Mr. Kemp's wide eyes met mine. He looked startled by the question, almost afraid to answer. "Were you there, Kaitlyn?"

I didn't want to respond. How could I admit that I'd seen exactly what had happened as I disgracefully hid behind the trunk of a tree? I'm sure my face had the truth written all over it, but I just couldn't bring myself to respond honestly, "No, I-I was just there after, and I heard students saying her name," my voice came out awkwardly and high-pitched as my eyes burst with fresh tears. Would he buy my answer?

"Kaitlyn, there are no words..." Mr. Kemp said.

I asked for clarification right away, "What do you mean?"

"She was *so* badly hurt...bleeding, bruised...and her head...oh, her head..." his voice faded away.

"What about her head?" Again, I asked for clarification. I hadn't seen anything specific about her head from where I was.

"Well, it was bleeding so badly...we tried to keep it wrapped up tight...she was completely unconscious...then the tremors..."

My jaw dropped and my eyes stared blankly past Mr. Kemp as my entire body became paralyzed with fear. His words rang in my head over and over...badly hurt, bleeding, unconscious, tremors. A large knot formed at the base of my throat as I tried to swallow and choke down the tears, but to no avail. Mr. Kemp knelt down in front of me and, even though he was in no position to be comforting someone else, he muffled his own emotions in an effort to keep me calm. To no avail. I couldn't control myself.

After a few minutes, I heard yelling and screeching coming from behind me where the door was.

"Kaitlyn!" Mrs. Blaine screamed my name as she ran frantically towards me. Eyes wide and bloodshot, hands shaking and black streaks of makeup down her cheeks, she wasted not a moment, "What's going on? Where is she? What happened?!" Her voice was laden with fear.

Mr. Kemp instantly stood up, quickly introduced himself and began to tell her everything he knew best he could. Emotional yet direct, it was evident that he didn't want to keep Mrs. Blaine in the dark any longer than she had already been. The words flew from his mouth and I watched her expression change from worry, to fear, to outright panic as she began to understand the severity of the situation. Her demeanour worsened by the second. Trembling in distress, she wailed and buried her head in her hands.

About fifteen minutes later, Mr. Blaine barged through the ER doors. I'd never seen him in such a state. He seemed angry, scared, sad and worried as hell. Instantly he demanded answers of his own. As Mrs. Blaine and Mr. Kemp retold the story yet again, I watched Mr. Blaine's grave reaction to the troublesome information. Over and over again, he said, "Oh no...oh no....oh no..." and ran his hands through his hair. I'd never felt so nervous in my entire life. She had to be okay, for me, for her family, for all of us. Right? The thoughts of what might be, what *could* be, were far too frightening to bear. After a while, as much as we wanted – *needed* – the situation to resolve, that couldn't have been further from reality.

I watched in horror as Mr. and Mrs. Blaine went through a vicious cycle of mixed behaviors. From nervously pacing the waiting room, to sobbing in each other's arms, to every so often letting out faint wails of fear, I saw them experience every parent's horror in those unsettling moments.

More time passed until, with much struggle, Mrs. Blaine lifted her head, gazed in my direction and softly asked, "Kaitlyn...w-were you there?"

How many times would I have to lie? Heart palpitating, I answered as steadily as I could, "No…just after." The words disgusted me.

We were in the waiting game now. The game where minutes feel like hours and hours feel like days. All we could do was wait – impatiently, hopefully, helplessly. As Mr. and Mrs. Blaine continued to battle their way through multiple stages of fluctuating emotions, I couldn't help but stare. They were in shambles. In my mind I pleaded over and over again…

Please let Rebecca be okay, please let Rebecca be okay, please let Rebecca be okay.

After phoning my parents and playing the painful waiting game for two hours, finally a doctor came to see us. I sat with my head in my hand, watching the doors from which I'd seen several doctors emerge in their blue scrubs. Suddenly, I perked up in my seat when I saw a tall, dark-haired man walk hastily through the swinging doors and head directly for us. The Blaines and Mr. Kemp followed my lead and turned their heads in the direction of my gaze.

"Hello, I'm Doctor Thomas," he greeted us.

"Hello, Doctor," Mr. Blaine responded, "I'm Rebecca's father."

They shook hands and the doctor let out a deep sigh before he began talking. "Rebecca is in critical condition," he explained, "among other more minor bodily injuries which I will explain in a minute, she suffered a severe traumatic brain injury. We will be monitoring her closely to check for swelling of the brain, which may lead to intracranial bleeding and excessive pressure. At the first signs of swelling, vessel or vein ruptures, or intracranial pressure, we will need to perform surgery immediately. I'd like to ask for your consent now so that in the event that we must perform an emergency surgery we're able to do so in a timely fashion, which is critical in such cases."

We were speechless. My tears returned as I tried to process every-thing the doctor had just said. Mrs. Blaine began to cry hysterically, while Mr. Blaine hastily put his arm around her. His bottom lip quivered as he struggled to find his words, tears now streaming from his eyes too. He cleared his throat and mustered up the ability to say, "Yes, Doctor, whatever you need. Please help her…she's our little girl."

"I know. I assure you we are doing everything we can," Dr. Thomas responded. He was very professional and I couldn't fathom for the life of me how he kept himself so calm and collected. "Rebecca has also suffered bad bruising and internal bleeding in various areas on her body. Her face is swollen with a few lacerations and contusions around her eyes as well. At this point, our primary concern is her traumatic brain injury. She is still unconscious, and in severe cases such as these, it is common for the patient to remain that way for several hours. Family only may go see her now, if you like."

"Oh, please Doctor, may I come too?" I blurted, uncontrollably.

"Are you a family member?" He asked.

"No…"

"It's okay, she can come with us, Doctor, if that's alright," Mr. Blaine stated.

"Oh, thank you, thank you, thank you Mr. Blaine," I responded in desperation.

He pursed his lips in an attempted, yet far-fetched, smile and looked back to the doctor for confirmation. "Very well," the doctor answered, "however, there is one other thing I'd like to talk to you about in private after you've had a chance to see her."

"Sure," Mr. Blaine answered. Then he turned to Mr. Kemp and reached out his hand in gratitude, "Mr. Kemp, I cannot thank you enough for what you did for our daughter today."

"It was the least I could do, Mr. Blaine. I'm only sorry I didn't get there sooner, and I'm appalled that such a horrific incident took place at our school. I assure you this matter will be dealt with. I don't know what else to say…" Mr. Kemp responded wholeheartedly and looked genuinely upset.

I pursed my lips and put my hand up in a subtle goodbye gesture to Mr. Kemp as the three of us walked towards the intensive care unit doors into the hospital.

11

ILL PREPARED

Have you ever found yourself in a situation where you know that no matter how hard you try and no matter how ready you feel in that moment to see what you are about to see, once you see it, you realize that there was absolutely nothing you could have done to prepare yourself? This is the only way I know how to describe what I saw in the hospital room that day. The girl lying in that bed – it wasn't Rebecca. With all my might, I stared, searching for some small part of her that I might recognize. Even though I'd so desperately wanted to see her, right then and there, I wished I hadn't asked to join the Blaines in that hospital room. It was far more than I was prepared to handle. Crushed, broken, battered – there she lay. My best friend. Her parents stood crouched over at either side of the bed up close to her head. Mrs. Blaine wailed and sobbed uncontrollably, while Mr. Blaine held her hand, kissing it over and over and over again while his tears trickled hastily down her fingers. I stayed put where I was at the foot of the bed, knuckles white as I gripped the metal baseboard. My stomach was in my chest, my head pounded, my legs shook and tears streamed steadily down my face. I couldn't speak. I couldn't move. All I could do was speed-ily replay the series of events that had taken place since high school had begun. My heart overflowed with shame, remorse and a sense of account-ability. I couldn't help but think...this was my fault!

I stayed in the hospital for a little while that day. I suppose it was late in the afternoon when Mrs. Blaine asked me if my parents knew of my whereabouts. I explained that I'd already spoken to them and that mom and I had texted a few times. I glanced back at my phone and saw the time. "Oh," I muttered, "my Mom will be here soon."

"Okay," Mrs. Blaine answered.

Just as I was stepping towards the door to go, Dr. Thomas returned and stated that he needed to speak with the Blaines in private. Good tim-ing, I suppose.

Mr. Blaine nodded and then much to my surprise, thanked me for being there and told me what a great friend I was to Rebecca. If only he knew the truth.

Home. At last.

Everything poured out of me in a state that can only be described as hysterical. No matter what I said, Mom and Dad were there. We sat together on the living room couch, their arms clasped tightly around me on either side. Their comfort, their sympathy, their love – it was exactly what I needed.

After I relayed every last detail I could remember of the doctor's medical jargon, I stopped and grew silent. Hanging my head low in shame, I debated whether or not this was it. Was now the minute when I would make my confession as a bystander?

Turns out it wasn't.

Ugh. Why hadn't I just moved? Taken even a single step? Done something – anything? I knew my parents could help me. Yet still, I couldn't bring myself to speak of it. Maybe it was denial, maybe it was fear, maybe it was the coward in me, but whatever it was, it perpetuated my silence.

"I'm so scared," I finally said, wiping away tears with the back of my hand.

"We all are," Dad said. "But, what's done is done and right now, your friend needs you to stay strong for her. The incident is now in the past and there is nothing you can do to change what happened. Remember your King Lear?"

"That way madness lies," I mumbled.

"Precisely," he answered proudly. My father was always so succinct, intelligent and deliberate with his speech. He had a way with words like few others and managed to catapult me back to sensibility more times than I can count.

Emotionally and physically exhausted from the day's events, I went to bed early that night. But I couldn't sleep. My stomach churned and my mind raced. Cold and unwelcome, the darkness of the night swallowed me whole. Images of Rebecca flashed through my mind as I thought back to our childhood days when we were happy and life was simple. My thoughts wandered through the years as we grew older together, auditioned for Leacrest, attended our first day of high school, the cafeteria encounter, Rebecca's nonchalance, my worry, the morning when Marcel told me of the locker incident, our meeting at the coffee shop, the party, and Rebecca's desperate plea for my silence. How I wished I could speak with her, talk to her. I wondered how she'd feel about our pledge now. Would she still want us to keep quiet after what happened to her, or now would she be more inclined than ever to do everything she could to make Chantel pay for what she did? The deeper I fell into my thoughts, the faster they raced through my head and the more uneasy my stomach became. Hours and hours went by and I could feel my physical – and mental – state worsen. When the first signs of daybreak appeared, I rolled over in my bed to face the light shining through my window. Perhaps the sunrise would bring me the comfort and hope I so desperately needed. As much as I wanted to lie there, to do nothing, to wallow in the fear of losing Rebecca, I jolted myself out of bed. Sleep or no sleep, I had a responsibility to be there for my friend. Just as Dad said, I owed it to Rebecca to stay positive, to visit her, to talk to her, to just *be* there with her – whether she was conscious of my presence or not.

I checked my phone. 7:00am. And about a million texts and missed phone calls from Jacob, Marcel and lots of other school friends. Forget them. Rebecca was top priority and I couldn't waste but a single moment texting people. After quickly throwing on a pair of jeans, a tank and a cardigan, I made my way downstairs. I could hear Mom's spoon clanking against her coffee mug and the rustling of Dad's newspaper in the living room. I barged into the kitchen, grabbed the phone and immediately began to dial.

"Good morning," I said hastily, "I'm going to visit Rebecca."

"Morning Kaitlyn," Mom answered. "Hold on one minute," she insisted as she walked towards me. Reaching her hand out for the phone, she asked, "are you calling the Blaines?"

"Yes," I responded, pulling the phone away from her. Five rings passed and then the answering machine picked up. "There's no answer," I reported, hanging up the phone. "Can you give me Mrs. Blaine's cell number, Mom?"

"Better not to call her cell since she's likely at the hospital," Mom responded. She had a point.

"Do you think it's okay if I go straight over there?" I asked.

"I think that might be your only option," Dad said as he wandered through the dining room door. "If you call their cell phones they likely won't pick up, since I assume they're at the hospital with her."

"Yeah," I agreed. "May I go then?"

"Yes, I'll drop you off there on my way to work if you can be ready in 10 minutes," Dad answered.

"Oh thank you, Dad!" I exclaimed, already halfway out the kitchen. I ran upstairs to brush my teeth and throw my hair back, feeling genuinely excited to see Rebecca. My body flooded with a hopeful confidence that there would certainly be marked improvements since yesterday.

A perplexed look on her face, Mrs. Blaine ushered me to stay outside. Confused, I removed my hand from the door handle and waited for her to join me in the hall outside Rebecca's hospital room. I saw her lips move as she said something to Mr. Blaine who then looked over at me through the glass. As the two of them walked towards me I knew instantly something was wrong. The door opened and they quietly closed it behind them.

"What's the matter?" I questioned. "How is she?"

Mr. Blaine spoke first. "The doctor informed us this morning that her brain has swelled since the incident. At this point, surgery is unnecessary, and in some cases, the swelling stops or slows, meaning that the patient never comes to require surgical intervention. But in Rebecca's case, at least right now, there still is a small chance she'll need surgery if the swelling continues. She has yet to regain consciousness," he concluded. After a long pause and a heavy sigh, he looked me straight in the eyes with an extremely troubled look on his face and said, "Kaitlyn, there is something else we need to ask you."

Alarmed by his tone, my heart beat faster right through my chest. They knew! Somehow our months of secrets had been revealed. I took a deep breath so as to prepare myself and then answered as calmly as I could, "What is it?"

Mrs. Blaine, eyes swollen and continuously dabbing her cheeks with a tissue to catch fresh tears, touched her husband's forearm and said softly, "Perhaps it's better if we show her."

Mr. Blaine grabbed his wife's hand and looked at her, "You're right." He turned towards me and said, "Kaitlyn, please come in."

Their reactions told me this was about something else entirely, which only made me even more apprehensive. Mr. Blaine opened the door and the three of us walked inside. He stepped to the right side of the bed and I resumed my place at Rebecca's feet. "Come closer, Kaitlyn," he said softly.

I made my way towards him as he placed his hands on Rebecca's arm, one on her wrist and one just above her elbow. Lifting her arm off the bed, he then rotated it slightly so that her palm faced upwards. I gasped at the sight. All along the full length of her forearm, Rebecca had a series of cuts. While some of the slash-like markings were scabbed over, most were faint red scars that were already far along in the healing process, which told me this hadn't happened during yesterday's attack. Not one was a fresh wound. Most were long and extended diagonally from her inner wrist to her outer elbow, others were short, smaller incisions and the rest fell somewhere in between. As I examined more closely, I noticed there were dozens of them, some even overlapping one another. "She's been cutting," I muttered under my breath.

"Did you know about this, Kaitlyn?" Mr. Blaine asked, sternly.

"No, Mr. Blaine, I swear," I answered honestly.

"Because if you did, I would expect this to be something you would have come to us about. We need you to be honest with us."

Although I was honest about *this*, I certainly hadn't been honest about the very circumstances which may have been the cause of it! Was it time? Should I come clean right here, right now in this hospital room? I could tell them everything. Every bone in my body ached to confess but my lips wouldn't budge. Instead, I faded from reality and was engulfed in a crashing wave of questions as I felt my heart palpitate faster and faster, beads of sweat beginning to form on my forehead. When had Rebecca started cutting? Why? Was it the result of unbearable torment from Chantel or something entirely unrelated? Had there been additional bullying episodes since the day between the lockers? How had I not caught even so much as a glimpse of the slashes on her arms until today? I wracked my brain about the clothes she'd worn recently. It was spring and over the past couple of weeks the weather had been unusually warm. Everyone had been wearing t-shirts and even shorts on some days, but I knew very well that with gashes like that, there's no way Rebecca would have been able to wear a t-shirt without someone taking notice.

"Kaitlyn!" Mr. Blaine's voice bellowed and my spiraling thoughts came to a halt.

"Yes..." I uttered a startled whisper, realizing by the tone of his voice that it wasn't the first time he'd called my name.

"Are you alright?" he asked.

"I'm not sure what to say," I responded, "I'm just – I'm shocked... and scared."

Mr. Blaine sighed, "I know. We are, too."

Desperate for answers, I probed a little further, "Could the doctor tell how long she's been doing this?" My gaze kept going towards Mrs. Blaine, the sight of her causing my concerns to deepen. She didn't mutter another word, only held Rebecca's hand in hers staring at her daughter in disbelief.

"He said likely a few months," Mr. Blaine answered.

Bit by bit, I was losing my friend. I began to realize that not only had our friendship begun to grow apart, but in the meantime, she'd also undergone a series of disturbing changes. I touched Rebecca's fingers and said aloud, "I wish we could talk to her...is the other arm the same?"

"Yes," Mr. Blaine answered.

"Does anyone else know?"

"No."

"You said before that her brain has swelled but that she can't have the surgery yet? What does this mean?" I prodded.

"Well, she's not yet stable enough for surgery, but her brain is still bleeding and it's not a good sign that she hasn't woken up yet," Mr. Blaine explained, repeatedly wiping his face with his hand. "The doctor's exact words this morning were that, quite simply, we can't do anything but wait."

And with that, there was nothing more to say. The room grew quiet, but it was far from peaceful. We stood and stared at her. I wished with all my heart for some tiny indication of a future recovery – the flicker of an eyelid or the twitch of a toe. Something – anything – would have relieved the constant worry, the devastation we all felt.

Hours passed but still Rebecca never awoke. When I returned home, I finally phoned Jacob. He couldn't believe his ears. Every time I was forced to speak about it, new emotions rose to the surface. Constantly thinking I'd have no tears left to cry, there were always more. Jacob sounded genuinely worried – for Rebecca and for me. He begged to see me, but my answer was no. In those days following that life-altering incident, I was consumed by Rebecca and her current state – whatever that state happened to be at any given minute. There was no time, let alone energy, to worry about anyone else. Not even my boyfriend. I knew he was just trying to be there for me, but I would have none of it. Was I intentionally trying to push him away? Not at all. But that's certainly what happened.

Marcel was next on my list. If there was anyone I could talk to, deeply and honestly about the specifics of Rebecca's situation, it was him. At least *he* knew of the prior incidents and although it pained me to think that I had been somewhat replaced, he was also the partner in what had become Rebecca's closest and most intimate relationship. I hoped he might be able to offer some much-needed insight.

We spoke for about an hour and a half. I felt bad for him because he had reached out to Mr. and Mrs. Blaine multiple times and although they kept him updated, they declined his request to come to the hospital to visit Rebecca. While I could only imagine what Marcel was going through, I also understood the fact that it had only been 24 hours and, had it been my daughter in that bed and in that state, I don't know if I would have wanted any additional visitors – boyfriend or no boyfriend.

I dove right in and spewed out all the information I had. It quickly became apparent that he was just as disturbed about the situation as any of us. I realized how much Rebecca meant to him, and although it only made the tears stream faster down my face, it was nice to hear. Part of me felt happy for Rebecca, that she'd found someone who loved her so much, and the other part of me sympathized with his pain – a young guy in love, forced to endure such a tragedy. We cried together, choking back tears between spurts of conversation as we shared our feelings and spoke dearly about Rebecca. About halfway through our talk, I shared the most recent, and possibly the most disturbing, facts. I described Rebecca's arms in detail – every size, angle, depth of cut that had engraved itself into my brain. After I finished the somewhat overly meticulous account of what I saw, there was silence. It was difficult to decipher whether this was silence from a guy who already knew what I'd just described, or who was entirely unaware. I quickly ruled out the latter as I thought to myself, when two people are in an intimate relationship, how could one be oblivious to such prominent marks? Even if Rebecca successfully hid her arms from the rest of us, how could she possibly hide them from him?

Finally, I broke the silence, "Did you know?"

Marcel sighed on the other line, followed by another moment of silence. "Can we meet?"

"You've got to be kidding me…you knew!" I exclaimed angrily.

"Kaitlyn, it's not that simple. Please, I'm asking you to meet with me so I can explain."

"Fine," I answered, as all kinds of judgments flooded my mind. What could he possibly need to explain? If he had even the slightest inclination, there was absolutely no excuse for leaving it unreported or at least speaking to someone – anyone – about it! My body grew hot as my anger rose. But then another thought dawned on me: who was I to think such thoughts? I'd known about Rebecca's bullying incidents for months and hadn't said a word! What made this so different? Shame and regret collided with fury and frustration. "Where and when?" I snapped.

"Uh…what about the coffee shop where you and Rebecca always go – the one by your house? I can get my Dad to drive me, I think. He's home right now. One second." I heard Marcel call his Dad and request a ride. "Okay, I'll be there in ten."

12

HIS TAKE

I'd been here before. Coffee in hand, leg shaking beneath the table, nerves getting the best of me.

Hands in his jean pockets, shoulders tensely high and eyes puffy, Marcel walked through the door in front of me. He quickly made his way to the table and sat down.

"You look awful," he said, a small grin making its way to his face.

"So do you," I jabbed back. "Grab a drink if you want. I need you to start talking," I said impatiently, knowing very well I couldn't wait another minute to hear what he had to say.

"Actually, I don't need one," he responded, nervously running his hands through his hair. "Here it goes…it was about a month and a half ago. Rebecca and I were –" Marcel hesitated, awkwardly. Quickly realizing this indicated some form of sexual activity, I nodded in understanding, "– together," he chose his words wisely so as to avoid any possible discomfort between us, "…and I noticed a few marks – cuts – on her right arm. I interrupted what we were doing because I was genuinely concerned about what

I saw. When I confronted her about it, she answered without hesitation, telling me her cat had scratched her."

"Oh Marcel, that's so –"

"I know – unbelievable. But Kaitlyn, in the moment, you have to understand that I wasn't thinking that way. Even though I found it odd, there was no reason for me to think otherwise at that point in time. I trusted Rebecca with all my heart. I love her so much," Marcel's voice gained a few octaves and I saw a tear stream down the left side of his face.

In an attempt to comfort him, I reached across the table and placed my hand on his arm. "I know you do," I said, sympathetically, "please go on."

"Well, after she told me it was her cat, I grabbed her arm to try and get a better look. And I did, but only for a second since because she quickly pulled it back and told me it was no big deal and not to worry about it. So, I stopped prodding. After that day, we were together a few more times but I never saw anything. Mind you, I wasn't exactly looking for anything either. I really never, ever would have imagined that she was cutting. Honestly, Kaitlyn…"

I stayed silent, trying to determine whether or not I believed him.

"The truth is, over the past few weeks I've barely seen her," he said sadly.

"What?" I responded, completely shocked.

"Yeah," he confirmed. "Why do you seem so surprised?"

"Uh…" I hesitated, trying to piece everything together in my mind before I spoke. Rebecca had been avoiding spending time with me, but most of her reasons involved Marcel. Had she been lying to both of us? "I've been trying to spend time with Rebecca over the last few weeks too… but she always had a reason why she couldn't. Most of the time, it was because she said she had plans with you."

Marcel's draw dropped and his brow furrowed. I could tell his mind was quick at work as he too attempted to put together the pieces of what had all at once become a troubling puzzle before us. At last he spoke, slowly and quietly, "And she told me she was spending time with *you*."

I let out deep sigh of distress as we locked eyes. At once, we'd come to a disturbing discovery about our dear friend and partner. If she hadn't been with either one of us, where had she been all that time? By herself? At home? Out somewhere? Cutting herself in the bathroom…the bedroom? I cringed at the thought.

"Chantel wasn't still bullying her, was she? Do you know?" I asked.

"Not that I know of. I really thought everything was over. I never heard of any other incidents from Rebecca or from anyone else at school."

"Me neither," I agreed. "But it doesn't make sense. Why would she have begun to hurt herself if everything was okay? If she was truly and genuinely happy, there would have been no logical reason for her to become a cutter. Something isn't adding up." I paused for a minute and reluctantly asked, "Can I ask you how your relationship was? I mean up until the point when she began to avoid spending time with you?"

"It was great," Marcel said confidently. "At least, from *my* perspective it was, and I always got the impression she felt the same way. We often had very open talks about our relationship and we'd each spill our guts." He smiled as he reflected on what was evidently a pleasurable past and then went on, "We'd talk about our love, our connection and how lucky we were to have found one another. Over the last few weeks, I've really missed her, you know? Even when I saw her at school, I felt as though something was different. She seemed cold and distant, but I didn't want to pester or bother her, and part of me thought maybe I was overreacting. There's no doubt that I'd taken her away from you a little bit and I respected the fact that she was spending more time with you - at least that's what I thought she was doing. Any ideas I had about feeling neglected or concerned, I justified it this way," Marcel shook his head in disbelief and then concluded, "I thought I was helping, not making matters worse."

I looked down at the table. "I just can't believe this is happening," I whispered, "she has to be okay...she just has to."

"She will," Marcel answered quickly. The confidence in his voice reassured me, and in that moment, I actually believed him.

13

WHAT'S NEXT?

Somewhere between conscious and unconscious, I lay there. Far in the distance, the phone rang. In my dreams, in my sleep, the sound of the phone provoked worry and nervousness. Even in my semi-conscious state, I knew the ringing of that phone was the sound of bad news – the sound of danger. I wanted to answer it, but the depth of my sleep was far too great. The ringing stopped and it was the silence that jolted me from my sleep. Just a few seconds later, Mom barged into my bedroom and the space flooded with light.

"It's Rebecca. We have to go right now."

I threw off my blankets, rushed out of bed and began opening cupboards and drawers, frantically trying to find something to throw over me in my disoriented state. Within a few moments, both Mom and Dad were in the hallway grabbing their jackets as I raced down the stairs to meet them. I threw on my spring coat, slipped my feet into the first pair of shoes I saw and ran out the door. We sat down inside Mom's car and she quickly reversed out of the driveway.

"Who called?" I asked.

"It was Shelly," she answered (Mrs. Blaine's first name was Shelly), "the swelling in Rebecca's brain has worsened and she is suffering from internal bleeding. She was just rushed into emergency surgery."

"Oh no," I sighed heavily. During the remaining minutes of our car ride to the hospital, the severity of Rebecca's situation began to really sink in.

I suppose I never truly thought it would come to surgery, or turn into a potentially fatal situation. When it's *your* life, when it's someone *you* know, you never think the worst. Something convinces you that it isn't so. Maybe it's a defense mechanism. Maybe you need to tell yourself everything will be fine because it's the only way you know how to cope. The thought of losing that person is unbearable.

For me, in that moment, I still wasn't anywhere close to thinking about Rebecca's death. I was merely coming to terms with the fact that she was about to undergo major brain surgery. I thought of her pain and wondered if she was at all aware of what was happening to her.

At 3:00am in the morning, ours was just about the only car on the road and we made it to the hospital in record time. As we raced through the doors, we saw Mr. and Mrs. Blaine pacing the waiting room, hands clasped tightly together. We embraced one another as we cried, and cried and cried.

After a while, our hold loosened and Mr. Blaine began to speak, "It's called a subdural hematoma," he explained, "it means a blood vessel or vein in her head was torn. This caused bleeding between her brain and the outer layer surrounding it and the surgery is performed to drain the blood from her head. We were in such a state of emergency because if the bleeding were to continue it could stop the flow of oxygen to her brain…and k–"

Don't say it! I screamed inside my head.

His eyes welled with tears as he struggled to speak. "Ki–" he tried again. He paused before concluding with something else, "The doctor did say this is a surgery that usually has positive outcomes. The doctors caught the hematoma in time, which is essential in these situations since the longer you wait, the greater the probability of missing the surgical window and letting the blood overtake the brain."

"How long has she been in surgery?" Dad asked.

"I'd say about twenty-five minutes or so now," Mr. Blaine answered, "we phoned you as soon as they took her in."

"How long do they anticipate the surgery will be?" questioned Mom.

"About four hours, they said – if all goes well, that is," Mr. Blaine answered.

"Yes, of course. Here, have a seat," Dad ushered the Blaines to sit down.

The next hour and a half went by brutally slow. Every minute was a struggle. Exhausted yet wide-awake, upset yet hopeful, we sat together in silence. Not a word was spoken, but the sentiment was clear. Love, support and strength held us together that morning. Finally, at 5:15am Rebecca's doctor emerged from the doors just ahead of us and we stood in unison.

"I'm happy to say that the surgery was a success," Dr. Thomas seemed genuinely pleased, and we all instantaneously expelled a huge sigh of relief amidst emotional sobs of despair. "Using what we call a burr hole technique we were able to drain the blood surrounding Rebecca's brain. Now, it is important to note that Rebecca is still in critical condition and given the severe head trauma she's suffered, there is a risk of complication. But, having said that, we will continue to monitor her very closely to respond quickly to any new developments if need be."

Mrs. Blaine burst into tears of relief as she hugged the doctor. "Oh, thank you, thank you, thank you!"

"Yes, thank you so much, Doctor," Mr. Blaine repeated, shaking his hand heartily. "When can we see her?"

"She's not awake yet, but you can go see her now if you like. However, she is in the ICU and we have a strict family-only policy following surgeries such as this one," Doctor Thomas explained, sympathetically.

"Doctor, these people are practically family to us. Would it be alright if we all went in?" Mr. Blaine asked.

Doctor Thomas was very reluctant but I think he could sense our desperation and eventually let us through. As we followed him out of the waiting area and through the ICU doors, I noticed the hospital felt different today. The lighting was brighter, the walls weren't closing in on me, and the people we passed in the halls appeared friendlier than the day prior. I knew the change was in me, not the hospital, yet I couldn't help but enjoy the uplifting alterations. Step by step, as we made our way to Rebecca, the cumbersome weight on my shoulders slowly lifted. Heel, toe, heel, toe… lighter and lighter. I even detected a small grin that had begun to take shape on my face.

I thought to myself, Rebecca is a fighter. If she could make it out of emergency brain surgery, she could make it out of whatever else was thrown her way. I felt strong and confident again. I began to picture what it would be like when she woke up, when she was finally fully recovered and we'd be able to talk. I'm sure everything would be different. After someone survives what she will have survived, life often takes on a new form. What meant the world to her before, may seem entirely insignificant now. She might have a brand-new outlook.

I imagined myself expressing every last emotion to her, telling her how much I'd missed her over the past month and how I couldn't bear the distance between us. She'd nod in understanding, hug me, and tell me she'd promise we'd spend more time together from now on. Our friendship would go back to the way it was and we'd be closer than ever. My entire body was warmed by the thought of what was to come. I couldn't wait.

We arrived at Rebecca's post-operative room and the doctor ushered us inside. She looked relatively the same as yesterday only today she had a large white bandage around her head. This was the first time my parents had seen her and while the rest of us managed to keep our composure, I could see Mom's eyes fill with tears as she gasped and covered her mouth with her hand. Dad shed no tears but I could tell by the expression on his face that he was gravely disturbed by the sight of our dear next-door neighbor. He embraced Mom as she quietly wept beside Rebecca's bed. I didn't cry that day. I was assured that the success of the surgery was a positive sign – perhaps the first – in Rebecca's recovery.

When I look back on that day, I often wonder if others felt hopeful in the same way I did. Were the Blaines confident that this was the beginning of her turnaround? Or was everyone rather nervous, anticipating further complications?

These are questions I've never asked. And likely never will.

The keys turned in the ignition and I could feel the car's engine rev beneath my seat. It was a chilly morning and the sun had only just begun to rise. We'd all had very little sleep and I felt thankful it was Saturday. As Mom backed the car out of the hospital parking space, I began to make plans for the day. I'd go home, call Jacob and Marcel to update them, catch up on my sleep for a little while and then return to the hospital in the late afternoon. If I planned my visit a little later in the day, there was a better chance she'd be awake, I thought to myself. My mind flooded with reveries of what our first words would be, how good it would feel to hear her voice again, how grateful I would be to know she was back, and how much relief I would feel after telling her how sorry I was for everything that had happened.

Mom's concerned voice broke me from my daydreams, "I – I'm –" she paused. "I'm utterly speechless," she muttered.

I put my hand on her shoulder from the backseat of the car, "Mom, this is a good sign. The surgery was successful and they drained the blood from around her brain. Her brain has been swelling for almost two days and now they caught the problem and fixed it. And she made it through. I think this is a really positive development. She's on the road to recovery."

"Her face..." Mom's lip quivered as she trailed off.

"I know. She's in very serious condition and she still has a long road ahead of her until she's made a full recovery," I responded sympathetically.

"I just can't believe other children were actually responsible for this. She's barely recognizable," Mom went on, "this sickening act is something you'd see in a movie – not in real life. Not in our city – not to someone we know and love."

I sat silent. She was right. As positive as I attempted to be, what happened to Rebecca was downright horrifying. But I was determined to put her welfare ahead of my feelings. I'd mourned the dreadful sight of her injuries two days ago. Now it was time to be strong. It was time to have faith, to be optimistic, to think affirmatively of her recovery.

"We need to be strong, Mom."

She sniffled loudly and wiped the tears from her face, "You're right. You're absolutely right."

"When we arrive at home, I'm going to phone Jacob and Marcel to tell them the news of what happened tonight and then lay down to sleep. In the later part of the afternoon, I'd like to go back to the hospital. Is that all right? I'll take the bus."

"Yes, honey, of course," Dad answered. "Don't worry, we'll drive you."

"Thank you," I responded appreciatively. I couldn't help but feel excited to see her again.

14

NEVER IN A MILLION YEARS

I put my fork down and finished chewing, "What do you mean?"

Her body was stiff, her eyes wide and her right hand clenched the phone tightly. She kept looking down as if it might ring again. Her gaze shifted first to the coffee table and then to me as she let out a grief-stricken scream the likes of which I'd never heard before. Repeating herself yet again, this time in a loud, bellowing, angry voice, she yelled, "She's gone!"

Feeling my heart begin to race, again I prodded, "What are you talking about, Mom!?"

The phone smashed to the floor and Mom rushed over to where I sat firmly embracing my shoulders with her hands, "She's gone! Rebecca's gone!"

I sat frozen in disbelief as my mind raced to comprehend what was happening. "I don't understand. She was better…she came out of surgery… she was recovering…"

"Oh, Kaitlyn," the sorrow in my Mom's face said it all. And Dad just sat there, stunned and speechless. I knew exactly what her words meant and yet I continued with my irrational, senseless inquiries. I'd been ambushed, bombarded so unexpectedly that I could make no sense of the situation. *Gone* – I repeated the word in my head as if it were the first time I'd ever heard it. Even though I cannot state the reasons for my actions or make sense of my behavior, I remember every tiny detail of that afternoon as if it were yesterday.

"Mom!" I shouted again.

"She's dead, Kaitlyn. Rebecca died..."

I felt my breath stop and my body shudder. My lips parted as I stared at her, stunned by the words I'd just heard. I glared into her eyes with such force, silently pleading with her – begging her to take back what she'd just said. She pulled me close to her and embraced me with all her strength. At first I didn't resist, but second by second, I began to feel myself lose control. My breath quickened until I couldn't breathe. Suddenly, I was smothered. The world was consuming me. I had to get out. Frantically, I shoved my mom away from me, stared at her intensely from a foot away and let out a blood-curdling scream so shrill that I couldn't even recognize my own voice. I remember my mother's face, full of shock, alarm and intense worry. When I had no breath left, my scream faded into the silent air. My body shook violently and my face grew hot. Feeling as though I couldn't stand another minute in that basement I turned suddenly and began to run.

I trampled up the stairs, down the hall and straight out the front door. In my socks I ran and didn't stop. All the way down the street, through the park and into the forest near our home. It was as though I wanted – *needed* – to get lost, to get away, to escape the nightmare that had become my life. Exhausted, maniacal and inconsolable, I felt myself lose my footing not too far into the forest. I tripped and fell hard to the ground, feeling my right knee scrape open on something jagged beneath me. My face in the fallen tree bristles and my body heavy, I lay there, gasping for air and bellowing in between breaths. I began to cry – my sobs loud and violent. Not a moment later, I heard someone approach from where I'd entered the forest.

"Kaitlyn…oh, Kaitlyn!" As much as I'd wanted to get away, there was no one's voice I was happier to hear than Mom's. She knelt on the damp ground by my side and lifted my head onto her lap. Stroking my hair and rocking me back and forth, she too sobbed. Every few seconds, I could feel another one of her tears drop onto my cheek and she'd quickly wipe it away. For so long we stayed exactly as we were. Neither one of us could move. When it began to grow dark all around us, slowly, my mom lifted me to sit against her and after a few more minutes, we peeled ourselves from what had now become the cold earth beneath us and stood up. Hand in hand, arm in arm, we plodded our way back to the house.

Home, in bed, closed off to the world and desperately trying to come to terms with the fact that my life would never be the same, my parents explained to me the medical cause of Rebecca's death. She died of what's called an ischemic stroke, which occurs when blood flow is blocked to part of the brain. They simply couldn't catch it fast enough. It happened so quickly…

After the explanations, consolations, hugs and kisses, there was nothing more to say. Nothing more to do. I was left alone. So, there I lay. Out of ideas. Lost. There were no more words to speak, nowhere left to run. Despite my attempts to escape it, to take it back, this was real. It was over and she was gone. The realization to which I'd just come made my body seize. I felt my eyes grow wide as I stared through the wall in front of me.

That moment was the first time I felt it – the indifference, the detachment, the unemotional takeover that would consume me for months to come. It was an evil, petrifying and uncontrollable feeling. I remember despising the sensation, and yet I succumbed, helplessly accepting the dark transformation. My blank stare continued – without a blink, without a budge. I slipped into what would later be diagnosed as Post Traumatic Stress Syndrome. My world grew dark. There I sat in my locked stare. Still, lifeless, emotionally numb.

Tired, but I couldn't sleep. Restless but I couldn't move. It was uncomfortable just to lie there in my own skin. Rushing through my head were flashes of horrid memories I so desperately wished would go away. Over and over again, I replayed every last event I could remember – even those unrelated to Rebecca's death. Every so often my thoughts would travel back to our childhood – our pre high school days...the days that were so much *easier* to remember. The start of Leacrest had been the beginning of a vile turn for the worse. If only we'd attended another school, maybe things would have been different. Chantel never would have entered our lives and Rebecca never would have been forced to deal with the painful, embarrassing and destructive reality of what it was like to be the victim of a bully. Never mind the victim of a bully, she was now the victim of a murder! They took her from me. The kicking, the punching – I winced at the thought of it all. Had they intended to kill her that day? Or was it a horrible accident they now regretted? Funny thing is, as I wondered what the answers would be to these very questions, I realized it didn't matter. Intentional or not, the outcome was the same. As I forced myself to replay the day in the schoolyard, I scoured my memory for the number of people I'd seen standing above Rebecca, forcing her into a state of complete unconsciousness one blow after another. Were there four, five, six? I remembered at least four if not five. One was most certainly Chantel – her long, prominently dyed, bi-colored hair was unmistakable and I remember it flailing about as she violently thrashed at Rebecca.

I paused my recount of the day to roll over and gaze outside. It was Sunday now, the day after Rebecca's death. As miserable as I felt inside, the sun shone brightly, the same way it had that awful day. If it were any other Sunday, I would have been outside rollerblading, walking, or sharing a patio coffee with friends. But none of that mattered today. Nothing seemed to matter anymore. I blinked rapidly, letting my eyes adjust to the light. As gorgeous a spring day as it promised to be, it was one that I knew I would only experience from the confines of my room. I stared through the window, shifting my focus from the tiny black squares of the screen to the baby blue sky beyond it. Back and forth, back and forth. I breathed deeply, forcing myself to think back, to remember who else had been there. Perhaps if I could recollect how the encounter *began*, I would be able to remember how many others had been there.

I walked towards the tree – the schoolyard's beloved, ancient, large weeping willow. It was gorgeous. Enormous and somewhat majestic in appearance, its sad, drooping branches were still leafless after the winter months. I'd almost arrived at the base of the tree, my favorite spot, where I thought I could catch up on a little English reading while I waited for my next class to begin, when I heard the commotion of abrasive, yelling voices behind me. I turned around to see Rebecca, who appeared to have been walking in my direction, when she too turned back to see what the yelling was about only to find that it was directed at her. I felt my stomach knot up again as I relived the pain of the last moments I'd seen Rebecca standing on her own two feet.

The most peculiar part of that day, a part that is sure to distress me until the day I die, is the fact that Rebecca and I don't share the same spare periods. That day, when I saw her walking towards what appeared to be *me*, she shouldn't have been there. She should have been in class. And yet she was there, she was coming to me. For what? Did she wish to tell me how much she missed me just the same as I missed her? Was she about to tell me all she'd been going through – the bullying, the cutting, the feelings of hopelessness and desperation that had so obviously begun to take over her life? Was she coming to me for help? Or had she simply decided to skip class? Perhaps she was on her way home where she could do the only thing she knew would make her feel better. Had she become so addicted to this self-destructive yet powerful sense of control that she couldn't make it through a full day of school anymore? I'll never know...

I saw her turn around to face her murderers as the pack of them hastily moved in on her. Five – yes, there were five of them. The assault began almost instantly after I'd turned around. It all happened so fast. Maybe *that's* why I hadn't run to help her. Maybe *that's* why I stood there. There wasn't enough time for me to make a difference anyways. No! I stopped myself. This was no way to think. Rebecca deserved better than that. She deserved a better friend than *me*. I was nothing but a coward, a useless bystander who did nothing to save the life of her dearest friend. What put me in a separate category from Rebecca's murderers? How was I so different? The fact that I didn't contribute *physically* to her death? Was that *it*? Not only did I not run to help, but I stood there and watched! How could I possibly forgive myself for this? And that wasn't all. What about everything else? Even if somehow, someway, my actions on *this* day were forgivable, were too my decisions on every other day? My awareness of Chantel's bullying and my agreement to stay quiet? My inability to report those acts of bullying that could have saved Rebecca's life? My complacency to blatantly go against what I believed in – what I knew was right? My spineless, gutless efforts to make a move when I ignored the discernibly negative change in Rebecca over the past month? If only one of my decisions had been different. If only I'd had the nerve to stand up just one time. It was vividly and painfully clear. I wasn't fighting against Chantel. I wasn't on the opposite side of the equation. My actions proved that we were, quite simply, on the same team. I wasn't her enemy…I was her accomplice!

My feelings of regret were overbearing. My self-hatred was palpable. My awareness of how helpless I was to change any part of my situation was incapacitating. Worst of all, no one knew. Except for Marcel, not a single family member or friend knew of the prior acts of bullying that had taken place against Rebecca. Her parents – oh, the Blaines! They had a right to know from where this act of brutality stemmed. But how could I tell them? How could I possibly admit that not only was I a bystander but that I also knew of prior incidents over the past several months, none of which I'd communicated or reported? They'd never look at me the same. Our relationship would be destroyed and they'd be overwhelmed with feelings of resentment. And I wouldn't blame them – not in the slightest. No, I couldn't possibly tell them. No one would – could – know. This, I would now take to the grave.

15

FOR REBECCA

Two days went by and I hadn't left my room. Mom and Dad came by countless times to check on me, relentlessly attempting to talk, force feed and provide comfort. I didn't even know where my phone was. Dead out of batteries somewhere, probably inundated with missed calls and messages. Since Saturday, I'd mustered up the ability to speak a little, but only enough to communicate the fact that what I really needed was to be alone. I could barely eat and refused all forms of communication from outside people. The Blaines, Jacob, Marcel and a few friends had even called my house several times. But I wasn't ready to face the world yet. Jacob, oh Jacob…my high school love. Now? I couldn't have cared less about him. It didn't matter anymore. Nothing did. Although I was aware of the fact that Rebecca was gone, it was still exceedingly difficult to accept. The secrets weighed heavy on my heart. As Mom and Dad came and went from my room, their faces were infinitely hopeful, anticipating that this would be the time I'd peel myself out of bed and come downstairs. As heartbreaking as it was to see their disappointment, I was helpless to the darkness that consumed me.

On Tuesday afternoon I heard a quiet knock at my door. I watched it slowly open and they both walked in, looking more hopeful than ever.

"Kaitlyn," Dad began, "how are you, darling?"

I continued my blank stare directly past him and didn't answer.

He continued, "Rebecca's funeral has been arranged and scheduled. The visitation is tomorrow and the funeral ceremony is on Thursday."

I know they expected that at least this news would warrant a reaction from me but still I remained quiet.

"Kaitlyn, did you hear me?" Dad prodded.

I nodded reluctantly.

"Okay, so you'll have to get out of bed tomorrow," Mom said, "We'll leave you be until the morning to get yourself ready. Do whatever you need to do," her voice was filled with worry and concern. She didn't wait for an answer but grabbed Dad by the hand and left my room.

As the door closed only a single thought came to mind: *I can't go.* How could I possibly attend? All the people, the crying, the tragedy...I couldn't – I wouldn't. I closed my eyes and let the anguish of my loss conceal me. Within what felt like only a few seconds, I managed to fall asleep. Since Saturday I'd barely had so much as a few winks. Every time I slipped under, I was haunted by nightmares of Rebecca as I relived the horror of her death over and over again. Only it wasn't a nightmare – it was my reality. The nightmares were nothing new, just an exact, detailed replay of the assault I'd witnessed. Kick after kick, punch after punch, one of the violent blows would eventually jolt me from my sleep, leaving me soaking wet as I gasped and panted for breath. And then for a split second, I'd forget. For a single instant, I'd fool myself into thinking it was just what it seemed...a horrible nightmare. Then life's heart-wrenching reality would set in yet again. My nightmare wasn't a nightmare at all. It was my life. And it was the *end* of Rebecca's.

This sleep was no different from the rest and within moments, I sat up violently, my hand over my chest as I instinctively tried to calm my body from shaking. As exhausted as I was, in this state it was almost better not to sleep at all. After I took a moment to recover from yet another distressing dream, I spun my legs around to the side of the bed and sat there, hands beside my hips, head hung low. Matted and tangled, my hair drooped down around my face. I hadn't showered in days and although the very thought of my filth revolted me, I made no effort to change my neglected state. It was almost as though, somewhere deep inside of me, I foolishly thought that if I just kept everything as it was, if I didn't change anything or make any efforts to continue on with my life, that this depressing reality would change. In some strange way, I almost felt as though even the slightest movement towards a mental or physical recovery on my part would be a downright betrayal to my lost friend.

I slowly stood on my feet and rolled my back up, one vertebra at a time. I rubbed my face with my hands and began pacing around my bed. I knew Mom and Dad expected me to attend the funeral, and yet the very thought of going frightened and overwhelmed me to the point that I didn't even know if I could muster up the strength to make an appearance. How could I explain my feelings? What could I do to make them understand how detrimental even the thought of leaving my room was? I spent the rest of the day worrying about tomorrow. When nightfall came, I lay in bed staring blankly into the darkness at ten, twelve, three, six … until dawn finally broke again.

After yet another night of intermittent sleep interrupted by vicious flashbacks, there was a soft knock at my bedroom door around seven.

"Kaitlyn?" I heard Mom's kind, empathetic voice ring through the door as she slowly opened it.

"Mom," I wasted no time in my attempts to defend my case. I decided the best way to begin was in complete honesty, "I can't go," I told her.

She walked into the room and came up close to the bed, kneeling down beside it so our eyes were level with one another, "What do you mean?" she questioned.

"I can't go to the visitation today," I said, clarifying my previous statement.

"Oh, sweetheart," she softly tucked my hair behind my ear, "you must go," she went on, "I won't let you miss this. I know in my heart it's something you'll live to regret terribly."

"But –" I persisted, "but, I can't. I haven't even been able to leave my room yet. The thought of seeing her casket, of facing all those people – oh, I really can't, Mom. I can't, I can't..."

"Shhh," Mom continued to stroke my hair, "Kaitlyn, you'll understand later, my dear. Please trust me. Rebecca was your best friend and I know it's impossible to let her go but you must attend today and tomorrow's events if not for closure, then at least to show respect to her family – and her life. Don't think of all the other people who will be there. Just focus on your friend. Remember Rebecca and use this as an opportunity to say goodbye in the company of friends and family who are also mourning her death and there to support one another."

Although it was the last thing I wanted to hear, I knew she was right. The time had come. I took a long pause before responding, "Just for Rebecca," I whispered.

Mom smiled softly, "Just for Rebecca."

For the next few minutes, Mom knelt on the ground beside my bed as I lay there holding her hand. Not another word was spoken but I knew she could feel my pain. In that moment, our connection was strong – stronger than it had ever been and for the first time since Rebecca's death, I didn't feel scared and alone. Even though it seemed as though she could read my every thought, my stomach flipped as the truth came rushing back – my secret. Everything I knew that she didn't. As Mom continued to stroke my hair, I felt compelled to tell her…to spill everything. After contemplating the confession in my mind for a few minutes, my time was up.

"Okay, sweetie," Mom began to pull herself up off the floor, "I'm leaving for work now and Dad will be leaving in a few minutes too. We're going to attend the 7:00pm visitation. Okay?"

I nodded.

"I'll be home around 5:00pm – I'm leaving work a little early today so we have time to eat before we need to head out. Can I ask you to please be showered and ready to go by 6:00?"

Again I nodded even though the mere thought of complying with her simple request exhausted me. I remember thinking, *how am I possibly going to do this today?*

But I did.

For Rebecca.

Nylons annoyingly pinching at my legs, my only conservative black dress hanging loosely from my weak body, my hair pulled halfback into a clip and a grim expression on my face, I sat at the kitchen table poking at my food. I felt frail and lifeless, dreading every moment of what was to come.

"Kaitlyn, please try to eat, honey," Dad said.

I looked up at him, "I feel so nauseous, Dad. I'm sorry…"

"You've barely eaten in days. We're worried about you." I could hear the concern in his voice.

"I know, it's not that I don't want to," I explained, "it's just that I feel so awful. I feel like I can barely move, never mind eat. Showering today felt like it was the hardest thing I've ever done in my life."

Silence fell over the table for a minute.

"How about just a few bites," Mom suggested.

My stomach told me it wasn't a good idea but I felt as though I owed it to my parents to at least demonstrate my small efforts to lead a normal life again – Rebecca or no Rebecca. I felt my hand tremble slightly as I dug my fork into the smallest piece of potato I could find on my plate. Feeling both sets of eyes watch my every move, I lifted the fork to my mouth, slowly put it into my mouth and forced myself to chew. The uneasiness in my stomach worsened but the look of approval Dad gave me was motivation enough to continue. Chicken, rice, carrots – I tried everything else on my plate. At the halfway point, it all went sour. A burning sensation began to form in my chest and I dropped my fork onto my plate as I swallowed several times. Knowing I couldn't hold it in, I jumped up from the table and ran down the hall to the bathroom, hearing my parents call after me from the kitchen.

Face white and eyes red, about ten minutes later I emerged from the bathroom. Placing my hand on the walls of the hallway for support, I slowly made my way back to my seat in the kitchen.

"Oh Kaitlyn, are you okay dear?" I could tell by the sound in Dad's voice that he almost felt responsible.

"I'll be fine," I said, reaching for the water glass. Part of me wanted to say I told you so, but I refrained. I looked up, first at Dad and then at Mom. Each of them had paused their dinner to look at me with utter pity. Their facial expressions instantly told me how terrible I looked. Taking a sip of my water, I looked away from them and into my glass. Finally, they began eating again and finished their dinner. I turned around in my chair to see the time on the clock behind me – 6:25pm. It was time to go.

The car ride was quiet and I think each of us was a little apprehensive about the evening. My fatigue was debilitating and my nausea took all my power to control. Needless to say, I wasn't in the best frame of mind upon our arrival to the funeral home. Given the extent of Rebecca's injuries, I knew the casket would be closed but part of me wished the opposite. I needed to see her, to feel her, no matter how painful the experience. I felt no sense of closure, no confirmation of the fact that moving on with my life was necessary.

How could I possibly do this successfully when I hadn't even had a chance to say goodbye? She'd been taken from me, snatched up and vanished from my life. When I left her side on Saturday morning after the surgery, I had felt confident in the fact that she'd surely make a full recovery. And yet I couldn't have been more wrong because the shocking news hit our household that very afternoon – a heartbreaking phone call that inevitably decided our lives would never be the same. Worst of all, I hadn't been there, beside her, with her, through the worst of it. I'd so foolishly assumed she'd come out of this, living a happy, healthy life. I hadn't taken so much as a moment to consider the fact that she might not. I couldn't have been more ill prepared for the news. I wished I could have at least been there… even if she wasn't conscious, even if she couldn't see me with her own two eyes, she would have been able to feel me, to know that I was there with her. Now, she was gone forever and I was expected to stand over her casket and bid farewell. Impossible. I wasn't ready – it was too soon.

In that moment, I'm not sure if I'd even yet come to terms with the fact that Rebecca really was gone. For good. Forever. The last few days my life had been nothing but a foggy, groggy mess. Today was my first attempt to live outside the confines of my room and I felt like a foreign species roaming the Earth. When Rebecca left, she took part of me with her. Confused, disoriented, weak and quiet, I walked through the doors of the funeral home with a shattered heart.

Almost instantly I was swarmed by people, the first of whom was Marcel. Oh sweet, Marcel. He looked almost as terrible as I did. Immediately, he took me in his arms, whispering in my ear how worried he'd been about me, how much he wanted to speak with me and how many times he'd called. I wanted to tell him I was sorry, to explain that I didn't want to hurt or worry him but that talking to someone – anyone – had been nothing short of impossible both physically and mentally, but my lips didn't move. I was afraid to speak, afraid that the moment I opened my mouth, instead of saying what I planned to say, that I would erupt in a blood curdling scream or that I'd start to cry so hysterically I'd need to be escorted from the building immediately. And so, I kept my lips pursed shut – for the full two hours we were there. Marcel looked genuinely hurt when I didn't answer him. He just stood there, staring into my eyes, waiting for me to say something. After a minute or so, his expression of expectation turned to one of grave concern and he asked me if I was okay. I nodded, but I knew he could tell I was nothing of the sort.

Next came Jacob. He hadn't even so much as crossed my mind since Rebecca's death. I wasn't expecting to see him there. He bombarded me – hugging me and kissing my cheeks. I couldn't move. I felt nothing. I didn't want his support. I didn't want his love. I didn't want any of it! I refused to hug him back or show any kind of affection. I can't explain it, really. It was just impossible. I looked into his eyes – his shocked, confused, sad eyes and I knew it was over. He didn't understand. He never would. How could he?

Throughout the course of the visitation, I could do nothing but focus my energy on staying calm and collected. I felt as though at any moment, I might collapse to the floor – exhausted, malnourished, heartbroken. There were so many familiar faces and yet, despite what Mom said, I didn't feel warmth or comfort from any one of them. In fact, I felt more alone than ever before. It made me sick to look around, seeing scattered groups of people talking, many of whom were even smiling and laughing amongst one another. The anger began to rise inside of me. This was no occasion for smiles or laughter – we'd just lost an amazing person in our lives…a daughter, a granddaughter, a best friend, a girlfriend. How I wanted to tell people to stop – to stop their attempts to make this a pleasant experience and to stand silently, miserably…like me.

The worst of it all was coming face to face with the Blaines. They stood there, embracing one another for support, looking as though if one let go of the other, they'd tumble to the floor together. In that moment, I forgot about my own sorrow and empathized with theirs. I'd lost a best friend, but tomorrow, these two parents would have to bury their own daughter. My heart ached as I stood there with them. Seeing them again only reminded me of my shameful secret and I couldn't help but feel responsible for their suffering.

I wished I could take it back. Rewind time. Make different decisions.

16

MY DIAGNOSIS

Surprisingly enough, the sofa was comfortable. It wasn't exactly the most attractive looking piece of furniture, with its dated floral pattern, but quite cozy. My hands clasped over my lap, I stared into the eyes of the person sitting before me.

"Tell me about the funeral," Dr. Channing's voice prompted me from the chair where she sat just a few feet away.

Reluctant yet acceptant of the fact that I needed help, I gathered my thoughts and proceeded to answer the question, "Ugh," I sighed, "it was terrible – just really, really awful."

"And why is that?" the soft, empathetic voice of the woman who I'd later refer to as 'my shrink' prompted me to expand on my rather vague answer. I was far from invested in the process and I lay there in doubt thinking that this was exactly how it happened on television – the psychiatrist asks the questions and the patient answers in as brief a manner as possible. Then the doctor continues by making simple, subtle, yet clever inquiries to keep the patient talking and the session progressing until finally, after numerous meetings, there is an incredible, earth-shattering breakthrough. Yeah, right.

As much as I didn't believe Dr. Channing was capable of giving me my breakthrough, I didn't mind that I was there. In fact, it didn't bother me in the slightest. But the truth of the matter was that since Rebecca's death, nothing did. Life had become monotone. I went through the motions and did what I was told, but that's where it ended. My vigor dwindled, my drive ceased to exist and my heart was numb. I didn't cry anymore. I wanted to, though. I wanted to feel something – anything – that would catapult me from this terrible hole into which I'd fallen so deep. I found it interesting that I was utterly and completely aware of my physical and mental state, and yet couldn't fathom how or when I would possibly be able to extricate myself from it. Distressed, depressed and heartbroken, no matter how hard I tried to stop the recollections, Rebecca's death never left my mind. The flashbacks consumed me to the point that homework was out of the question and sleeping had become close to impossible. Yes, I needed to be here – this I knew for sure.

"I was nauseous and upset and there was an enormous lump in my throat that made it impossible to swallow," I explained, "I didn't say a word to anyone – I was petrified that I'd completely fall to pieces if I did. Now that I think of it, I don't remember much of either event, to be honest," I squinted my eyes and furrowed my brow as I tried to recall some small part of the events, "It's so blurry..."

"That's alright, Kaitlyn," the doctor's smoothing voice came again. "Apart from Rebecca's visitation and funeral, how have you been?"

The dreaded question, *how have I been*? What do you mean, how have I been? Terrible! Why else would I be here? Deep down, I wanted to be honest. I wanted to tell my psychiatrist everything – all the secrets that haunted me. I knew if I was completely open and honest, the likelihood of her providing me with *real* help was far greater. Yet here I was, thinking, contemplating how I could sidestep my dilemma. To be honest, at that point in time, I'm not sure that I really wanted to be helped. And so, I told her what I could without lifting to the surface all my buried secrets of the past seven months. There was a long pause as I carefully planned my answer.

"Kaitlyn?"

"Well, I haven't been good, Dr. Channing," I answered honestly, "I find I can't stay focused on anything, and school is particularly difficult. Over the last week, when I'm there, I keep replaying everything. When I turn a corner in the hallway, I always think I see her and then I remember..." the words were so hard to say, "I remember she's gone."

"Yes," Doctor Channing said, "please go on."

"Even right now," I continued, "even speaking to you – it's so, so difficult. Talking about her...every word is hard to get out. It's as though I'm struggling, fighting not to remember because it's just too painful and yet everyone wants me to talk about it, which only forces me to relive the pain that I'm trying to forget."

"I know it's hard, Kaitlyn, but it is very important that you're open with me. You're doing a great job," she said encouragingly. "What about sleeping? Are you able to rest at night?"

"No, not really," I responded, "I'm lucky if I fall asleep for a few minutes here and there but that only means that instead of thinking about Rebecca, I dream about her. Then I jolt awake drenched in sweat and gasping for air."

"I see. And what about extracurricular activities? Your parents tell me that you're a dancer but that you've stopped dancing. And how about friends, have you been trying to get yourself back to a normal life?"

Instantly, I became irritated, "Normal?!" I jumped up from the sofa, looking at Doctor Channing in disbelief. "Normal? You think my life will *ever* be normal again?" I screeched. "My best friend is gone! She did nothing wrong and she's never coming back! Does it really sound as though my life will *ever* be 'normal' again? It won't." I stared at her coldly for a minute and then sat back down.

Doctor Channing paused and then said calmly, "Don't you want to dance? Or see your friends or do any of the things that you enjoyed before Rebecca died?"

At first, the question seemed easy to answer but as my thought process deepened, it became more complex. My initial reaction was, no. Not one single part of me had the desire to do anything I'd done before. Rebecca's death made it all seem as though it didn't matter, that it was all nothing more than a useless, waste of time and that I was undeserving of it – of all of it. But then I imagined it: dancing in the studio, music blaring and body fully invested in the movement. Dance had always been an outlet for me. No matter my mood, no matter my life's circumstances, whether I was positively or negatively charged, I was able to channel that energy into my dance. And it felt great. It made me sad to think of how much I missed that feeling. If only I had the strength, if only I had the will, the emotions I felt for my loss would undoubtedly give me the ability to dance like never before. *That* form of therapy would be far more effective than having talks with some stranger. "No," I finally answered, "I can't be happy. It's not right. Rebecca is gone which means she can never do any of the things that she loved. So why should I?"

"But you're still here," Dr. Channing went on.

"I shouldn't be," I muttered under my breath. Part of me wanted to let it out – to tell Dr. Channing at least *one* of my many deep secrets. Why should I be happy when it was my fault she was gone? The bystander who hid behind a tree and did nothing gets to be happy but the victim doesn't? And how about the vow of silence I'd taken to honor Rebecca's wishes just because I didn't have the guts to do what I knew was right? No way. Happiness wasn't in the cards for me.

"What do you mean by that, Kaitlyn?" Dr. Channing's voice stirred me from my inner thoughts.

Huh. What a useless waste of time and money to be in a therapy session where the therapist didn't have a clue about the kinds of thoughts that were really going on in the patient's mind. Still, I held on tight to my secrets. I cloaked my inner body with them like a blanket, now immersed in the pain that was so familiar it had almost become comfortable. Dr. Channing didn't know the depths from where I spoke. Not only was I a silent bystander, but I was also aware of two other incidents – plus there were probably more. As badly as I felt about my decision not to interject the altercation that day, my regret ran much deeper than that. It began on the very first day of high school and continued to the day she died.

Finally, I found my words. It wasn't much, but all I could say was, "Never mind."

The remainder of the session was bleak. Although I forced myself to answer her questions, my responses were short and lacking any real detail. I was repeatedly engulfed in flashbacks of Rebecca and on several occasions, Dr. Channing was forced to repeat her questions in order to obtain an answer from me. At the end of the session, she asked me to wait outside while she spoke with my parents. After walking me to the door and opening it wide, she called for Mom and Dad to come in.

They both set down what were likely a couple of magazines that were barely worth reading and rose from their seats. Waiting rooms are always the same, I thought to myself. Whether you were at the dentist, doctor, psychiatrist…they all contained an awfully poor selection of reading material – all those magazines dropped on one's front door step that would ordinarily be used as fire starters or blue-box fillers, yes, these were the magazines in the waiting rooms. Mom brushed my face with her hand as we crossed paths and asked if I was okay. I nodded in confirmation and walked a few more steps to the closest chair, picking up one of the crappy magazines as I nestled in for the wait.

After about half an hour, the door opened, Mom and Dad walked out and Dr. Channing called my name. Me again? I placed the magazine on the table and began to make my way towards her office. Although we didn't exchange words this time, I couldn't help but notice the grim expressions on my parents' faces and it looked to me as though Mom had been crying.

"Is our session not over?" I inquired, curiously.

"Actually, it is, Kaitlyn. The first two hours we spent together were meant to provide me with some indication of exactly what you're suffering from. In most cases, this two-hour assessment allows me to accurately identify your situation," Dr. Channing explained.

"You mean like a diagnosis?" I asked.

"Yes, essentially," she paused before continuing. "In your particular case, Kaitlyn, I believe you're suffering from Post Traumatic Stress Disorder."

I was puzzled, "Doesn't that only happen to people who have survived a near-death experience or who have been involved in traumatic situations themselves? Like people who come back from the war?"

"No. PTSD is quite common in people who have lost someone very close to them," Dr. Channing responded.

"Are you sure I'm not just going through a period of sadness or something?"

"Well, PTSD is part of that, but there is much more involved. It is a form of anxiety and some of the most prevalent symptoms of PTSD that you are presently experiencing include flashbacks, nightmares and episodes of reliving the event, all of which are preventing you from carrying on with your usual day-to-day activities. You also expressed to me your inability to *feel* anything right now, how your frame of mind reflects the notion that nothing really matters and that you don't care about the things you once did. Your avoidance of social situations, insomnia and concentration difficulties I believe are all attributable to PTSD. The good news is, I am confident that I can help you through this."

I wasn't quite sure how to react. I didn't feel frustrated, upset or angry. Just the same. It didn't matter to me. I stayed quiet and let Rebecca flood my mind yet again.

"Kaitlyn?" I heard my name ring loud and clear in Dr. Channing's soft and soothing voice, "Are you okay with that?"

Unsure what she was referring to, I said, "I'm sorry, what?"

"I said I'm going to bring your parents back in now and the four of us will discuss the best steps forward together," she smiled warmly.

"Okay," I answered, indifferently.

It was a strange moment for me. I was aware of the significance of my diagnosis and yet, I felt not even the slightest bit of emotion. Dr. Channing had just perfectly described my every symptom, explaining how my daily actions correlated to the PTSD diagnosis. The nothingness I felt in that very instant was, in fact, one of the symptoms. It was peculiar to know that the very way I felt was a direct result of the diagnosis I was given seconds before and still I was without the power to change my reaction. I *wanted* to care, I *wanted* to feel, I *wanted* to have some kind of response. But it wasn't in me.

17

DEEP IN IT

Have you ever suffered from depression? As a child you never think in a million years that you might answer yes to such a question. In fact, you probably think you're impervious to a lot of things. Unless you lose control.

Depression was, by far, the most dreadful experience of my life. Imagine with me for a moment that a dark, evil power has swallowed you whole. Every day, it feels as though you've hit rock bottom. Until tomorrow comes. Sometimes it's hard to breathe, your chest is heavy as it weighs down on your ribs and sinks into your heart. On some days, you don't even want to open your eyes. The brightness of the world is too much to take in. Smiling is completely out of the question. You can't even if you wanted to – which you don't.

Everything feels weak – your arms, legs, fingers and toes – almost as though you haven't moved a single bone or muscle in months. All you want to do is lie there, wherever your comfort spot is, be it your bed, the family room couch or that old, tattered armchair in the basement. You want to be in a space that is quiet, usually dark and most importantly, non-threatening. The funny thing is, what non-threatening meant to you before, means nothing now because everything is a threat. Even concerned parents or loving friends who move oceans just to be there for you – it is their very presence that you come to dread the most.

When you hear a knock at the door, your heart jumps and your stomach turns. Who will it be this time? That split second of uncertainty before the door opens is enough to throw you into another bout of anxiety and personal torment. The last thing you want to do is speak. The effort it takes, even to whisper a handful of words, is exhausting. And yet, no matter how tired you are, no matter how many days it's been since you had a decent night's sleep, you can't catch forty winks. Your racing mind keeps you from resting. You lose interest in everything that once mattered. What other people think of you is of no concern and neither is what you think of yourself.

Feelings of sadness and guilt overtake all others, leaving no room for pleasure, happiness or even complacency. Relationships fall apart and good friends are lost. To concentrate on anything besides the very thing you're trying so hard to forget is impossible. And this makes participation in any form of real life activity unmanageable. So, you go back to your safe place. Here you stay because this is all you know how to do. Your safe place doesn't scare you, judge you or let you down. It doesn't ask you questions you can't answer or urge you to do things you're simply not ready for. It lets you be. Still and alone.

You lose your sense of time, mostly because it doesn't matter. What difference does it make whether it's Monday, Friday or Sunday? No matter what day of the week or what time of day, you feel exactly the same. Nothing is different. No changes, no new developments, no positive improvements. To say you're in a rut is a profound understatement. This isn't a rut – it's a complete and utter malady, and one over which, at most times, you have no control.

I think depression is such a difficult disorder to overcome because the very tasks you must perform in order to improve are the very ones that seem to be completely out of the question. For me, it was my awareness of the disorder that made it all the more difficult to handle.

Shortly after my PTSD diagnosis, I was diagnosed with depression. I understood the disorder, I acknowledged its symptoms and recognized the existence of those very symptoms in myself. I had no choice but to deal with my ill mind, as it told me every day that this was insurmountable. It was my mind that sucked me back into the black hole, that told me it wasn't possible, that convinced me I was here to stay. Over the course of the two months I suffered from depression, I began each new day thinking, wondering if today would be the day I would progress, move in the right direction, make some tiny indication of improvement. But the weight on my chest, the weakness in my body, the heaviness of my eyes – they held me back. The pain of my loss reminded me that I didn't deserve to be better, I was unworthy of a normal life. If she couldn't have it, then neither should I.

Devoid of energy, emotion and purpose, I was just another girl with a broken heart. I could barely even recognize myself. Once a strong, willful and vibrant personality, I was an effervescent girl who could never get enough of the socialite lifestyle. Being alone was out of the question before. I'd accept the company of others any day, any moment before I'd sit alone. And now? The polar opposite. A lost soul. A forlorn teenager. In those darkest days, the world had me conquered. How could anyone expect me to beat this? All my confidence, all my determination, all my gusto…I'd lost it somewhere along the way. I had not an ounce of faith in my ability to overcome this hardship. It was taking me, consuming me, one cell at a time.

Each day I felt as though I'd sunk a little deeper, a little further into my black hole. It was the guilt that overtook me. Every day it gnawed away at me...I could have done something, I could have spoken up, I could have told someone. And if, just if, I had done so, everything might be different. I might not be lying here alone, traumatized and depressed. And Rebecca, oh sweet Rebecca – she might still be with me.

No. This is where I deserved to be – alone, closed off from the world, only my guilty thoughts to accompany me. I missed my dear friend terribly. As I lay there in my room, I slowly and inevitably rotted away, one minute at a time.

Weak, unhappy and forever hopeless.

18

IF IT WEREN'T FOR THE ANTIQUE STORE

The sun was so bright it burned its way right through my sunglasses. Useless, I thought to myself. Arms crossed, lips pouting and back slouched, my body language was clear: I didn't want to be there. I was so angry I could barely contain myself. Out of my safe place, every moment felt like a struggle. Why had they made me go with them? I was sure to make their Saturday road trip miserable. If I were them, I certainly would have left me at home.

It was May 24th and a beautiful day indeed. It had been just over two months since Rebecca's death and just under two months since my diagnoses. I continued to see Dr. Channing but with little success. At first, I still attended school but after a little while, even that became too difficult. My attendance began to drop and It had been almost two months since I'd been to Leacrest High. Given my state, my parents decided it was best for me to focus on my recovery, at which point I would re-enroll and determine how best to make up for lost time.

Marcel had left me a voicemail telling me that Chantel, along with the other kids who'd physically assaulted Rebecca in the schoolyard, were each charged and would be going to trial. When I initially heard the message my first thought was, who cares? Sure, hopefully they receive the justice they deserve to pay for what they did. But it wouldn't bring her back. Those disgusting people had taken Rebecca from us forever. Marcel reported that they'd also been expelled from school, which I found to be quite comforting since student expulsions were anything but common in bullying news. Bullies went unpunished and victims were left to simply "deal with it". Oh, how I despised that phrase. "Deal with it". Sure, and look how Rebecca dealt with it? By cutting – by harming her own body as a result of the cruelty of other people because she simply didn't have another answer. And me? I didn't know how to deal with it either. Perhaps I'd rot away in my bedroom, never amounting to anything. I certainly wouldn't be the first person to let their life go to waste.

As the car bounced along the dirt roads, it quickly became apparent that the city was long behind us. A road trip indeed, only this particular adventure wasn't exactly my idea of a thrilling experience since the final destination was one in which I had very little interest: an antique shop. Great. My parents on the other hand, lived for this and they'd taken me a number of times as a little girl. I could only vaguely remember, but of course in those days I would have had my toys and coloring books to keep me occupied. This time there were no distractions – just me and my thoughts, same as any other day. But on the road, out in the open, I was miserable. They'd ripped me from my safe place and I did everything I could to show my disapproval of the situation. On several occasions, both Mom and Dad tried to start a light and amicable conversation with me but my one-word answers made it abundantly clear that I wasn't the slightest bit interested.

"Almost there, Kaitlyn," Mom said excitedly. It felt like such a long time since any of us had spoken during the ride that her voice startled me a little.

"Great," I replied snarkily. I immediately felt badly afterwards.

"Listen," Dad's voice came authoritatively, "we've accepted your attitude for about an hour and a half. That snide comment will be the last. Understood?"

"Yes," I replied solemnly.

Within the next few minutes, we'd arrived. As terrible a state as I was in, I felt badly for my conduct. For the last few months my parents had done nothing but console and support me through what was supposed to be my recovery. Progress up until now was slight, if that, and yet still they were unconditionally supportive. From my therapy appointments and my inability to attend school, to my unwillingness to participate in any of my extracurricular activities and my insistence on complete solitude, my parents were forced to endure it all with me. The car came to a stop and we each exited one by one. As we walked across the parking lot towards the antique store, I stopped.

"Mom...Dad," I said, waiting for them to turn around. "Listen, I'm sorry. For everything, but especially for my behavior today. To be honest, I just really didn't feel comfortable coming."

Mom replied understandingly, "We know, honey. But it's good for you to get out every now and then, even if you have to force yourself at first."

I nodded, "Well, since I'm not interested in antiques, would it be alright with you if I just waited outside and got some fresh air while you shop around?"

They looked at one another and Dad shrugged his shoulders, "I suppose that would be fine," he answered.

"Okay," I said, giving them my best attempt at a smile. "I'll be right over there," I said, pointing to the wooden steps off to the side of the front doors.

With that, they turned and walked away, quickly disappearing through the doors ahead. I stood there for a few moments in the parking lot, letting the sun's rays beat down on me – a feeling I hadn't experienced in some time. It felt good. I stepped slowly in a circular formation, taking in my surroundings from every angle. As I walked towards the steps where I promised my parents I'd be, I noticed that to the right of the antique store off into the distance, was a school. It had an unusual, quaint appearance just like the antique store and certainly didn't look anything like Leacrest or any other city school to which I was accustomed. In fact, the only giveaway was the name on the front of the building: Hope Hills Public School. Elementary, I concluded.

I walked closer and assumed the spot on the wooden steps, just where I said I'd be. I gazed at the school in the distance. It seemed barren and empty. At first, I thought it must be a weekend, but then I remembered it was Tuesday. Mom and Dad had taken a day off work, which evidently explained why a mid-week day felt more like a Saturday or Sunday. Mind you, one day just fizzled into the next in my world, so it was easy to lose track. I rested my elbows on my knees and flopped my chin into my hands gazing out into the distance at the school. It looked like a warm and welcoming place – not like my school. I don't think I'd have a problem attending *this* school, I thought to myself. It was beautifully situated, made of red brick that gave it a homey kind of appearance, and even the name made it sound as though it was a friendly place.

I was broken from my thoughts when a loud bell rang out from the school. Recess! Within seconds, children swarmed the perimeter. Front, back, side doors – they seemed to come from everywhere. I felt myself smile. It was the first in a long while. From afar, I watched them. Some stood in groups talking, others ran around frantically playing what appeared to be a game of "tag", and the littler ones screamed in excitement as they raced for the playground. It was such a pleasant sight and I was instantly reminded of my own elementary school days, when life was easy and I was happy.

Over the next little while, I lost myself in the playful antics of the children when suddenly something caught my eye. A small group had formed way outside of the general crowd and stood in the very back corner of the school grounds. They stood just inside the chain link fence and it appeared to be a confrontation of some kind. I squinted, trying to make out what was happening. Still struggling to see, I slowly rose from the wooden step where I sat and began walking towards the schoolyard.

Still far in the distance, yet closer than before, I was able to make out four male figures. As I gradually moved in on the scene, step by step, the image became clearer. One boy had his back up against the chain link fence and the other three boys stood opposite him. On the opposing side, there appeared to be one leader and two more secondary figures. The leader stood out in front, closer to the boy against the fence. Occasionally I'd see an arm or leg fill in the gap between the boy and the other group but I couldn't make out exactly what was happening.

Right foot, then left, I stepped closer. Now the boys were about a hundred feet away from me and there was no question about what I saw. The one against the fence was being taunted by the other three – although most of the aggression appeared to come from the boy who assumed the lead role, while the other two laughed on either side behind him. The leader jabbed at the poor boy against the fence – lightly punching him, pushing him further into the fence and kicking dirt on him. Again! There I was – *again* witnessing an act of bullying. It wasn't just Leacrest High, or just girls, or just the other select stories I'd heard on the news. No, this was *everywhere* and *everyone* was a possible target. Hope Hills Public School was no different. Why weren't the teachers in the yard more observant? How could they be missing this right in front of their eyes!?

My steps grew quicker until I found myself running towards the boys in the schoolyard. No way, no how – I wasn't going to be a bystander this time. And then suddenly, the bell rang and the bullies at once dispersed and ran towards the school. Saved by the bell. I slowed down but then noticed that the young boy against the fence had quickly hid behind a tall birch tree at the very corner of the play yard to avoid going inside with the rest of the students. My mind quickly flashed to the day in the school yard when I too had chosen a tree as my shield from the reality before me. The boy slouched into the corner of the fence and buried his head between his knees. I continued to run towards him but stopped myself several feet away, knowing very well that he likely wouldn't want to have anything to do with a complete stranger. And rightfully so.

From far away, I called out softly, "Are you okay?"

Slowly, the boy lifted his head and looked around, puzzled by where the voice had come from. His face was wet with tears. He couldn't have been more than ten years old. It took him a few seconds, but then he saw me. I couldn't help but notice how adorably handsome he was. I racked my brain to think of why anyone would want to bully this cute, young, innocent boy? Rebecca flashed into my mind and I remembered instantly that there didn't need to be a reason. Rebecca was a tall, beautiful, smart girl, and yet somehow, she'd become the target of a demented young student at Leacrest.

There was a long stare before he got up and ran in the direction of the school to get away from me.

"Please! Don't be scared, I want to help!" I screamed after him.

To no avail.

He yanked open the door and disappeared into the school. Just like that he was gone and there was nothing I could do about it.

Or was there?

I ran as fast as I could back to the antique store, flung open the door and quickly scanned the interior for my parents. Out of breath and understanding the urgency of the situation, I frantically explained what had happened, and more importantly, what needed to happen next.

And then we were three.

Nervous as hell but feeling a strong sense of moral duty take over my body, I rang the doorbell of Hope Hills Public School.

A woman's voice rang through the intercom, "Yes, how can I help you?"

The lump in my throat choked me up for a second. Quickly forcing it down with a huge swallow, my answer came, "I just witnessed an act of bullying in your schoolyard. May I speak to someone?"

Silence.

"Uhhh…" she hesitated. "Please give me a moment."

"Of course," I replied.

In about three or four minutes, a woman and a man came to the front door of the school. The man walked in front, pushing the door with his hip to open it.

"Hi there," he started, "I'm Principal Jenkins. Lilian just told me you saw something in our schoolyard. I'd like to hear about it, but could you first tell me who you are?"

I can't remember the last time I felt so nervous. This was my chance – a real chance to make a difference in someone else's life, or many lives, or an entire school. I didn't know where to start, how to come across, or what might be the best opening line to make them listen to me. So, I started from the beginning.

"My name is Kaitlyn Lee. I was sitting outside the antique store over there waiting for my parents when I saw a bullying incident take place in your schoolyard. My best friend died two months ago as a result of bullying."

That got their attention. Looks of horror and empathy took over their faces and they uttered sincere apologies to me.

All I could do was nod, as I felt my stomach churn and my eyes well. Hearing myself announce the most horrifying fact that had completely overtaken my life was crippling and liberating all at once.

For a second, we stayed quiet. Then everything came out. "Her name was Rebecca and she was only 14 when she died," my voice began to quiver. "She was wonderful," I went on, "a really amazing friend who played the saxophone and we had just started high school together last fall. You know, it wasn't just one incident. There were lots – I'm not even sure I know about all of them. The first was just a minor thing in front of our cafeteria. A few months before she died, she was pinned hard against the lockers at our school and had a horrible bruise on her neck for weeks afterwards. It was around this time that she began to pull away from me. I tried to make her talk, to tell me about what she was going through, but she closed herself off. When we finally met for coffee one night, I really wanted to report her bully to the principal and tell our parents. But she begged me not to open my mouth to anyone about what happened. I was so desperate to keep our friendship and I was scared that if I went against what she said, I'd lose her forever. So, I listened. I ignored my instincts and dismissed what I knew was right. A little while later, she was attacked again, this time outside in the schoolyard and there wasn't one, but five of them," I gasped for air as I burst into tears. A few seconds later, I concluded by telling them, "And then three days later, she died in the hospital."

I wiped my face frantically and looked up. They had each shed a tear with me.

Feeling oddly supported, I went on.

"I've seen firsthand the worst of what can happen if bullies aren't stopped. It gets out of hand fast. And it's not worth it. If one of us had spoken up and tried to do more, Rebecca might still be here. That's why I rang your doorbell. I cannot – and *will* not let history repeat itself and I will not be a bystander crippled by silence yet again. I saw an incident in your schoolyard and I know it's my duty to inform you. I'm doing this for the boy who was victimized, for everyone else those kids will bully if I say nothing, and for the bullies themselves because if I speak up, at least this gives them a chance to make a change."

"You're right," the woman uttered softly.

"Several boys cornered another boy in the back of the schoolyard during recess. I saw pushing, shoving and punching to his body. I couldn't make out what they were saying from where I was, but I imagine it was anything but nice," I explained with a sigh. "I can describe the boys to the best of my ability, if you like."

"Yes, please," said Principal Jenkins. He then glanced over my shoulder and looked back at me. "Are those your parents in that car?"

"Yes," I answered.

"I'd like to bring you in to our office where we can gather a full report from you," he said. "Do you think they would mind if you came in? You're welcome to bring them with you."

"That would be great," I answered, knowing how badly I could use them by my side right now.

I ran to the car, told them what was happening and the three of us entered Hope Hills Public School a few moments later. It took some time, but I appreciated Principal Jenkins' thorough approach because it was a strong indication that he took bullying matters seriously. I got the feeling that this wouldn't be just another file cast aside on a busy principal's desk.

When the process was complete and my job was done, my parents and I were escorted out of the school. As we walked to the car, I felt lighter on my feet. I could smell the freshness of nature in the air again. I noticed the sky's vibrant blue hue. That little smile came back again and I realized how much I'd missed this feeling. It was the feeling of, quite simply, being me.

Dad put his arm around me and gave my shoulders a squeeze. "You did a good thing in there, kid."

My grin widened as I answered, "Thanks, Dad."

Mom grabbed my hand tightly and smiled as she said, "I'm so proud of you."

I wasn't cured. I wasn't fixed. Life wasn't magically okay again. But it was a start.

On the long car ride home, although the beginning was filled with recounts and explanations of what just happened, I was appreciative when we let the dialogue come to an end. My parents played music from the sixties at just the right volume for me to enjoy the background tunes, and let my mind immerse itself in a sea of transformational thoughts. At first, there was a period of realization. What I just did was speak up. Exactly what I should have done for Rebecca, but didn't.

I messed up. I should have told someone. I messed up. I should have told someone. The profound words echoed in my head. While I did feel fresh guilt and shame, my mind was in a completely different place. I started to ask myself, *So what? So what? What are you going to do about it NOW?*

Although he didn't know it, the bullied boy in the schoolyard that day changed something within me. Our lives had collided – unexpectedly and yet ever so importantly. For the first time in months, I felt a tiny bit like me again. My body felt more alive. Somehow, someway, I had shared Rebecca's story with complete strangers, shameful secrets and all. Not even my parents knew all of what I was able to tell the receptionist and principal at Hope Hills.

The tone of my thoughts changed to be transformative.

As terrible a truth as I held inside until that day, I felt liberated to have finally told someone...anyone. Rebecca's story was powerful. I told Rebecca's story to show them, to *prove* to them, that sometimes it doesn't just go away. Sometimes the bullies don't stop. Sometimes awful things happen, and to prevent them, we must take a stand – as victims, as bystanders, as friends, as teachers, as principals, as parents...as strangers. What if maybe, just maybe, what I did today saved that boy in the schoolyard from years of future torment and misery? What if it inspired the receptionist and principal to begin an anti-bullying initiative at the school to inform and protect their students? If the story and my choice to speak up had the power to make even the smallest impact today, right here and right now, on a single young boy, on a single school – then why couldn't it do the same for other schools full of students?

My energy began to rise further and further in the back seat of the car that day. Mind racing and my heart beating faster and faster by the minute, I knew I was on the brink of something big – something huge. Although my secret truths were painful to admit, they had the ability to give other people a perspective that no book, movie or classroom lesson ever could.

That was it!

My new-found purpose.

Rebecca's story needed to be told. And I would be the one to tell it.

19

THE START OF
SOMETHING REAL

My mind was moving far quicker than my mouth and it was impossible to get my words out fast enough. The expressions on their faces told me how astounded they were by my sudden change in demeanor. I rambled on and on. It was as though I was a sieve, letting every granular story seep through. My shame and hesitation melted away and I told them of all the terrible secrets I'd held in for so long. Rebecca's prior incidents and my cowardly moments as a bystander who said nothing in the schoolyard. And then finally, I got to my plan. *The* plan. The plan to make a difference, to start something that would not only carry on Rebecca's name but that I passionately hoped would also make a positive impact in the lives of other bullied students at Leacrest. If Rebecca was bullied that meant other kids were too. After about half an hour of nonstop stories, explanations and future plans, I was finally finished. I breathed a huge sigh of relief and ended with a simple, straightforward question, "So, what do you think?"

Mom and Dad looked at one another and remained silent for a minute.

"Wow," Mom started, "that's a lot of information to take in all at once."

I chuckled a little from the backseat. "I know." This was certainly one way to make the dialogue return in the car that day.

"First of all," Dad chimed in, "It's nice to have you back, Kaitlyn."

I smiled from ear to ear.

"And I think your plan is a good one – a great one in fact. It has purpose and value and I can tell you're passionate about it already. And in this world, following your passion leads to happiness and personal fulfillment – and that's infinitely important," Dad went on. "Whatever you need – guidance, advice, assistance in getting your word out – anything at all, your mother and I are here to help you anytime. I want you to know that," he concluded.

"That means a lot, Dad. Thank you so much," I replied genuinely.

But there was more. "Now, can I regress into a more serious response to what you just told us and discuss your secrecy for a moment?" My heart skipped a beat as Dad's tone changed to one of concern and disillusionment.

"Yes," I replied, "I know you must be so disappointed in me. And I am of myself too, which is why I couldn't muster up the courage to tell anyone until this very minute. Not a single soul knows about the fact that I saw those five girls attack Rebecca in the schoolyard. And the only other person who knows about Rebecca's other incidents is Marcel," I continued on to describe my meeting with Rebecca at the coffee shop – how I had strongly suggested that we tell our parents and report Chantel to the school principal. I left no page unturned and no detail unexplained. Brutally honest about the fragility of our friendship, I explained how I felt Rebecca slipping away from me, and how I feared that if I didn't comply with her requests, our relationship would crumble. I told them I was confident that there were more incidents than even Marcel and I knew of. Even though they were already aware of the doctor's discovery of Rebecca's cutting, I told them of my strong belief that Rebecca was gradually and detrimentally broken down since the start of high school. I explained that I felt so traumatized by Rebecca's death because I believed it was me who was to blame. Not Chantel, nor the other four attackers – *me*. If I'd only followed my intuition and done what I knew was best for Rebecca, she might still be alive. I expressed that up until today, up until this very point in time where I finally believed that I'd found a reason to continue, I didn't feel worthy of living.

I couldn't have asked for a better reaction from my parents. While I could tell they were severely disappointed and expected more out of their daughter in such a situation, their compassion, understanding and sympathy shone through. They made me painfully regret the fact that I hadn't told them sooner. We addressed my lapse in judgment to stay silent, and my experience as a bystander who now had a moral and legal obligation. That part scared me, I'll admit. Given the fact that there was a huge investigation surrounding Rebecca's death, it was clear that now I would need to play an even larger role than if I were still merely the "best friend to be questioned". My parents explained that I would need to come forward immediately to the police and provide a statement, not to mention the truth I owed the Blaines. Even though there were uncomfortable and serious conversations, what I remember about that car ride home was our empowering, future-focused dialogue. I think Mom and Dad understood that forward talk would be much more beneficial than backward reflection, for which there would be plenty of times to speak but now wasn't one of them. We planned, we discussed, we brainstormed and we bounced ideas off one another. First and foremost, I had to be re-enrolled in school and my parents said they'd place the call to Principal Cabello as soon as we returned home. We'd need to arrange a meeting with him and possibly my teachers as well in order to determine how I'd return to class, what material I'd have to learn, tests I'd need to take and missed assignments I'd need to complete. Timing could be tricky since it was May and school would be over in a little over a month.

This also meant that I'd have to work quickly to deliver my story before summer arrived. Oh, but it would be far more than a story. I would create a *campaign* – yes, a campaign to speak out against bullying and to tell the school of my heartbreaking story that maybe, just maybe, could have had a much different ending if I weren't yet another bystander in the war against bullying. What would I call my campaign? How would I promote it? Ideas raced through my mind as slowly, piece by piece, my plan began to take shape.

A special energy filled the car on our way home. Each of us talked over one another in excitement, incapable of waiting for a break of silence before we spoke – probably because we knew one would never come! Even though none of us knew quite what we were on the brink of, I think we all felt its significance. Home couldn't come soon enough since that would mark the very first actionable step of my plan: the call to Principal Cabello. As soon as we walked through the door, I ushered Dad to the phone. He couldn't so much as take off his jacket before making the call. After a few brief moments on hold, I heard him connect with the principal and arrange a meeting between he, my parents and I for that coming Thursday, just two days away. Moments after the phone call was made, my parents bumped up my Saturday appointment with Dr. Channing, thinking it would be a good idea for me to discuss my secrecy and my breakthrough with a professional who could provide independent guidance and advice. I would see her tomorrow. Even though I now felt strongly in my ability to pull out of my PTSD and depressive state, I also knew it wasn't going to become a full cure without help. I would continue my therapy – anything to help me jump the new hurdles ahead of me, and ensure the success of my plan. And my revelation did not come without fresh complication and dutiful responsibility. Rebecca's fatal attack now had a witness – a witness who hadn't come forward until now. I'd kept this terrible secret inside all these months. Now it was out. And it was time for me to step up. Step forward. Do what was right and what was required by law, and handle all of the repercussions that might come along with it.

As for right now, this minute? It was time to get to work. I hustled upstairs to my room and froze in the doorway. In a single instant, my excitement was drained and my motivation lost. All-too-familiar feelings of depression, guilt, sadness and indifference surged through my body. No, no, this was all wrong. I couldn't begin my plan here – the room in which I'd laid for months in the depths of my horrid condition. Absolutely not. Change was essential. I immediately turned back around and ran downstairs.

"Mom, Dad!" I exclaimed. "Will one of you *please* take me to the paint store?"

They exchanged looks at one another and then turned back to face me. Simultaneously, they asked, "Why?"

"My room is a depressing hole. If I'm really going to turn myself around, I need an interior makeover."

"Let's go," Mom answered.

I smiled and spun myself towards the front door. We grabbed our things and were on our way in a flash. As we made our way to the paint store just around the corner, I said with confidence, "Yellow."

"What's that?"

"The room needs to be yellow," I explained, "that was Rebecca's favorite color. And it's said to provide clarity in decision making and protection from lethargy and depression." I paused for a split second and smiled, "It's perfect."

Mom looked over her right shoulder and smiled back at me, "It most certainly is."

The positive events of that day only continued at the paint store. Everything just seemed to fall into place. Finally! At last I knew exactly what I wanted. It all made sense. There was no time to continue my vicious cycle of deliberation, overanalyzing or regret. I knew exactly what to do, and while I didn't know precisely how to get there just yet, I was confident I'd figure it out as I went along. I chose the most warm, beautiful, vibrant yellow I could find. I'd never painted before so Mom instructed me on all the supplies I would need, from paint brushes and rollers to tape, plastic covering and trays. Within about half an hour we had everything we needed.

In my mind, there wasn't a moment to waste and the second we arrived home, I began to load all of the bags upstairs. Mom and Dad helped me move my furniture out of the room – except for the bed, which we moved into the center and covered with plastic. When we were finally prepped and ready, they each offered to help me paint, but much to their surprise, I declined. I knew in my heart this was something I had to do on my own. I was excited to be alone with my thoughts, to think of the days ahead, to plan my new endeavor and to remember Rebecca in a more peaceful, healthy way. They wished me luck and left me to it.

Stroke by stroke, I watched my room transform before my eyes. With each movement of the roller, I felt my inner darkness fade; with each swipe of the paintbrush, the weight atop my shoulders grew lighter. The process was enlightening as it propelled me forward in mind, body and spirit. Calming music rang through my ears from the iPod dock in the corner. Graceful and comforting, it brought me to a deeper level of awareness. I was able to hear the subtlety of the instruments and appreciate the vocals in a way I never had before. There was a warmth that flowed through my body as my icy loneliness began to melt away. My dark hole was dissipating and I could see the light again.

That night, before I lay down to sleep, I sat on my bedroom floor and began to scribble my thoughts down on paper. From campaign names and awareness pieces, to phrases I thought I might say in a speech to the school – it was now in writing. I must have been there for hours because by the end of the session, I had an entire notebook full. The thoughts I'd brainstormed with my parents earlier that day or conjured up on my own as I painted, now had their own visual component in my master plan. The words on the pages made it real, made it genuine. I even created an action plan so I had a crystal-clear idea of exactly what needed to be done to bring my campaign to life. The first step, and likely the most painful, would be my meeting with the Blaines. My nerves had already begun to build. It was too late now but tomorrow evening, upon their return from work, I would make my way over to confess everything I knew and all that I'd been hiding since September. I was well aware of the fact that it might be the most difficult conversation I was yet to have but the necessity of it was beyond measure. I continued to remind myself that at the end of my confession, I would have *good* news to report – news that I dreamed would maybe, just maybe, result in a future victim saved, a life spared and Rebecca's name forever honored.

Although I thought of Rebecca every waking moment since her death, that night was the first time I spoke to her. I talked to her as though she were still there, right in front of me. Imagining her safe and comfortable, I began to make my connection – wherever she was. I lay in bed, in the center of my room and whispered a few words aloud to my long-lost friend.

"Rebecca...I'm sorry I haven't been here for you since you left. I couldn't face it all until now. I couldn't imagine living my life without you. The guilt of my secrecy has torn me to pieces and before today, I was confident that I couldn't - wouldn't - move on. But now, I have a plan. And it's all for you. The only way I know how to live without you is to tell your story. I miss you every day. Sometimes I forget, just for a second that you're not coming back. And in that instant, it's as though I'm relieved, I'm happy and I feel whole again. But then I remember. And when I do, I go through the horror all over..." I began to weep as I continued. But they weren't tears of sadness - they were tears of relief. I had finally found the strength to let her go just a little.

"I cannot tell you how sorry I am for not running to your rescue that day in the schoolyard. It will be something I regret for the rest of my life - and I have to live with that. I could lie here and give you reasons for my cowardly actions - but I refuse. There is no reason good enough. And I'm sorry you struggled in silence, that you felt alone, that you thought there was no one to turn to and that you resorted to self-harm to find the answers. I can't imagine what that must have been like..." I paused for a few moments in reflection before I spoke again.

"I'm going to speak to your parents tomorrow and I'm going to tell them everything. And I want you to know I'm going to be brutally honest. I'm going to tell them about our night at the coffee shop, about the other bullying incidents, about how I felt you slipping away from me. Don't be upset and please don't think of this as a betrayal. I had every intention of taking my promise to the grave, but it's not right. I must be open - first to your parents, and then to everyone, to our entire school. Because yours is a story that has probably already happened to others somewhere in the world, and that will likely repeat itself. It's a story that can help people. I truly believe that. And by telling your story, I can carry you with me through the days ahead. You're not alone anymore. Now you have a purpose, you belong, and you are loved. I think your story already helped a poor boy out in the country today. But I don't need to tell you that, I know you were watching. It was you who gave me the strength to finally speak. Just as we helped him, I believe we can help so many others. The number doesn't matter though, because even if I can help one – just one – then it's worth it to relive the pain of the recollection." And with that, I said goodbye, "Goodnight by dear Rebecca. Talk to you soon."

I closed my eyes. And for the first time in months, I slept. No interruptions, no nightmares, no sudden jolts from my sleep. At the crack of dawn, the sunlight woke me through my window.

20

FINDING MY STRENGTH

The next few weeks were about getting on my feet. As a matter of fact, I mean this quite literally, since I'd spent the last two months lying on my backside, locked away in my bedroom hardly ever seeing the light of day. Although my long-term plan was clear as day and even easy, the way I saw it, I knew the first few steps to get me where I needed to be would be difficult. The first of which, was my confession to the Blaines.

Although dreadfully challenging to face, particularly from an emotional standpoint, this was the step that I found to be most important. Not only did it play a critical role in my personal recovery but it was also essential to my commitment to specific values and morals as an individual. The lying, the secrets, the withholding of valuable information from two people who deserved to have every tiny detail surrounding the loss of their child so that maybe, just maybe, a little more sense could be made of the situation – all of this needed to be put to an end. Although I kept busy, planning and conjuring up new ideas to implement my awareness campaign in honor of Rebecca, the day passed as slow as one would expect. The Blaines worked full time during the day and had returned to their jobs about a month ago after taking some time off to mourn the death of their daughter. I decided to be as respectful as I could in terms of timing and planned my arrival at their doorstep for 7:30pm – just after dinner hour.

Ding dong! I rang the bell. Mr. Blaine answered the door. He looked weak and tired and dark circles drooped below each of his eyes. He almost appeared older, as if the death of his daughter had aged him. "Kaitlyn!" he exclaimed, seeming genuinely happy to see me and quickly ushering me inside. His excitement instantly triggered the flutter of butterflies in my stomach as a rush of nerves and shameful guilt swept over me. How I dreaded what I was about to say...

For Rebecca, for Rebecca, for Rebecca. I repeated the words over and over again in my mind. Without wasting another moment, I spoke up, "I'm here to talk to you and Mrs. Blaine. Is she home?" I inquired.

"Yes, certainly," he answered, his expression dimming slightly as he took notice of my serious tone. "Shelly!" Mr. Blaine called up the stairs for her.

Within just a few seconds, she began to walk down the stairs to the front hallway where we stood. I felt my jaw drop as she slowly and unsteadily made her descent. She must have lost 20 pounds – and she certainly didn't have 20 pounds to lose! Ever so thin and weathered from the storm that had uprooted their lives, Mrs. Blaine looked as though even walking was difficult. Her eyes glazed over as she approached me. Shakily placing her hands on my shoulders, she spoke softly, "Oh, Kaitlyn, it's nice to see you. How are you doing?" There was concern in her voice.

"I'm much better, actually," I answered. "I'm here because I need to talk to you both about something extremely important and difficult," I explained, "but first, please let me ask how the two of you are doing." I paused, uncomfortably. "I don't quite know what to say...I can't imagine..."

An overwhelming sadness in his eyes, Mr. Blaine answered as honestly as he could, "You know, Kaitlyn. There are just no words for what we're all going through. Right?" he prompted me for reassurance.

I couldn't have put it better myself. There really was no way to describe it. "Yes," I answered.

"Come," Mrs. Blaine spoke, guiding me into the living room. "Would you like something to drink before we sit down?" She asked kindly.

"No, thank you."

And with that, we began. For a long while, I talked without interruption. I explained everything: the minor incident on the first day of school, the confrontation between the lockers, the party and finally the brutal beating that led to her death. I told them about our night at the coffee shop, how I wanted us to get help but how I felt compelled to honor Rebecca's wishes. I was honest about the day in the schoolyard, how I hid cowardly behind the tree and watched the attack from afar, never mustering up the courage even to make the slightest attempt to step in. I assured them that I understood the graveness of my silence and its associated repercussions and how I would now need to come forward to the police immediately.

It was a painful and emotional conversation that felt as though it would never come to an end. Tears streamed from my eyes while the Blaines each looked at me in shock, sorrow, even disgust at times, sobbing in their individual chairs just a foot or so in front of me. Fearful of their reactions, at times I wasn't sure whether or not they would hear me out to the end. At one point, Mr. Blaine stood up, as if sitting in his chair had become unbearable while he struggled to process the troubling information I spewed out in droves. I think if I were telling the story to an impartial listener, it would have been easier to control my emotions but the fact that I was telling it to the heartbroken parents of my dearest friend only made matters worse. At times I fought to get the words out, but still I pressed on. I kept reminding myself of the fact that once I managed to communicate the most painful and shameful stories, then it would be time to tell them of my plan to carry on Rebecca's name. And *this* would make it all worthwhile. I was careful to tell them of all the details, in chronological order, leading up to her death.

After this, I went on to tell them of my personal shame and deep regret that I hadn't done something – anything – to save her. How I felt responsible for her death and that up until yesterday, didn't think I would ever be able to leave my bedroom and face the real world again. I told them of my PTSD diagnosis, depressive state and extreme emotional instability, how I saw a therapist three times a week and would continue to see her for a long while yet. I told them how sorry I was – for not listening to my instincts, for not coming to them with all this information before it was too late, and for not making the move I should have made that day in the schoolyard.

Finally, I was finished. I had said everything I wanted to say about Rebecca and myself, but I hadn't yet told them of my campaign. I felt they needed a minute to digest the weighty confession I had just unloaded.

At first, there were a few moments of silence. Mrs. Blaine looked positively furious as she continued to sob quietly in her chair and Mr. Blaine reached across to hold her hand as he stared downwards at the floor. As I looked closer, I could tell there were tears streaming from his face too. My heart pounded as I waited for a response – any response would do! Yell, scream, demand me to leave the house, anything...the suspense was killing me.

The silence persisted.

After a few moments, something I never expected occurred. Mrs. Blaine rose from her chair and threw the glass in her hand ferociously against the wall to my right. The smash was enough to curdle my blood. What had I done?

Fists clenched and face crimson red, Mrs. Blaine glared at me from across the room. "How could you keep this from us for all these months?" she spoke quietly and slowly, only a greater indication of how angry she was. It was as though every word was difficult to say because all she wanted to do was scream at the top of her lungs.

I didn't answer. What could I possibly say?

Her raspy, intense voice came again, "This is our daughter. Our daughter! She's gone and all these months we've been searching for answers. And you had so many of them! How could you, Kaitlyn? How could you?!"

My glance shifted to Mr. Blaine and although he appeared equally troubled by Mrs. Blaine's conduct, he dared not speak a word.

She was right, but I responded the only way I knew how in an attempt to correct my awful mistakes. Fearful of her next move, I put my hands up imploringly in front of me as I spoke, "Mrs. Blaine, I am so, so sorry. Words cannot express how sorry...but I'm here now. I know it's not much. But I'm here. I feel as though you can't stand the sight of me right now – and I don't blame you – so I'm going to say this next part fast and then I'll leave and I won't return until you tell me you're ready to see me. I plan to carry on Rebecca's name – to make a difference by telling her story."

Mrs. Blaine's brow furrowed in confusion and Mr. Blaine squinted his eyes in search of more answers.

Onward I continued, "I'm going to create a campaign in Rebecca's honor. I don't have all the plans in place yet but I see the campaign as an awareness initiative that brings bullying stories out into the open, that inspires students to stick together and stand up for one another and that lets participants show their support with paraphernalia like t-shirts, wristbands, headbands, hats and phone cases."

Slowly but surely, their grim expressions began to change. And ever so slight, a tiny glimmer of hope appeared. I told them of my revelation the day prior, with the boy in the schoolyard out in the country and I gave them an overview of what I'd pieced together so far for Rebecca's campaign. It wasn't much, but it was something. The vision was there. Although faint, the smidgen of change I saw in their faces only made me more excited.

And that was it.

I got it all out.

I did what I had come to do.

And with that, I slapped my hands on my knees and rose from the sofa.

"It makes me so sad that I was the cause of even more tears. Trust me when I tell you that if there was anything I could do to take back my actions these past nine months, I would do it. I miss her so much, it hurts. And even though every day is scary without her, this feels right. I know her story can help people. When it's all said and done, I'm doing it for her. I'm doing it for Rebecca – to carry on her name, to work hard for change and to hope with all my might that by sharing her story, I can make even the tiniest difference in another person's life."

I slowly walked between the Blaines, through the living room French doors and into the hall. To my surprise, they followed me there. I turned around to bid my farewell and although neither of them spoke a word, their expressions, through all the anger and hurt, told me I had their blessing.

I took a deep breath. Ahh, there it was: the unforgettable, mouthwatering smell of freshly baked muffins. For a split second, I was saddened by it. My heart ached for Rebecca. I forced myself to acknowledge my pain and push onward, so I gave my head a little shake and stayed focused on my plan of action.

I knew returning to my classes would be difficult. I had a lot of schoolwork to catch up on, not to mention the fact that even as I took my first steps down the main staircase of my high school I could already feel people staring, pointing and huddling into groups whispering to one another about who I was and what I was wearing. It came as no surprise that my t-shirt was causing a bit of a stir in the hallways. It was Rebecca's favorite color, a bright vibrant yellow. On the front, in big, black, bold letters was the slogan and title of the campaign I had carefully and strategically put together prior to my return: *Time to Talk*. And on the back, there was a picture of Rebecca with the words *For Rebecca* below it. It was my favorite shot of her. I'd taken it last summer when we were lying in the grass in my backyard talking about how excited we were to attend the same high school in the fall. Rebecca's blond hair fell loosely just below her shoulders, a huge smile lighting up her face. It was perfect.

My chin held high and an undeniable sensation of confidence surging through my body, I walked into the cafeteria for one of those hot banana muffins I'd missed over the last few months. As I removed the wrapper and took my first bite, I was surprised to see Marcel sitting with Jacob of all people just a few tables away from the cafeteria door. They weren't really friends before...perhaps they'd grown close over Rebecca and I? Walking straight over, I sat down in the empty stool between the two of them. Not yet realizing who I was, Marcel turned his head to face me. Jaw dropped wide open, he let out a loud scream and hugged me with such vigor that my muffin flew out of my hands and onto the floor behind him. It was such a heartfelt greeting that my lost muffin was the last thing on my mind. Marcel let go and stared at me in disbelief. Next came Jacob. While he appeared somewhat reluctant and obviously hurt, he approached me nonetheless and I couldn't believe how good it felt to hug him again. I knew there were probably a ton of things the two of them wanted to say to me (by no means all of which were good) but no words came out of either of their mouths. I couldn't help but chuckle to myself at the sight of them both.

"I know," I said, feeling as though words or no words, I could read their every thought. "I was going to call you guys but I wanted to surprise you instead. And let me tell you, that reaction was worth the wait!"

"I – I –" Marcel stuttered, "I can't believe you're here…"

"I know," I repeated again.

"How are you, Kaitlyn?" came Jacob's concerned voice to my left.

I looked over at him and smiled, placing my hand over his. I'd forgotten how good-looking he was. It was obvious how heartbroken he was after I'd just stopped all contact with him like it was nothing. I can only imagine how that must have made him feel, of course, he had no idea the depths of what I'd been through either. Maybe one day I'd have the opportunity to tell him. Now certainly wasn't the time or the place, and besides, I was on a mission. So, I chose my words carefully, "I'm okay," I responded, nodding my head. "*Now*…" I emphasized the word, "*Now* I'm okay." Pausing for a moment before continuing, I tucked my hair behind my right ear. "And I'm here with a plan," I stated.

"A plan?" Marcel sounded curious. "What kind of plan?"

I'd been leaning over the table, my arms crossed in front of me so I knew neither of the boys had seen my shirt. I pushed my stool back, took off my bag and sat up straight for them to see. They each looked down and then back up at me with mixed expressions of intrigue and confusion, followed by pride and adoration as the wheels in their heads started turning. I could tell the moment when they figured it out. Then to solidify their suspicions, I spun myself around in my stool to show them the back. I stayed there for a moment and then swiftly turned back around. Jacob looked stunned and Marcel's eyes were welled with tears.

"Wow," Marcel whispered under his breath. "Kaitlyn…"

"It's a great picture, isn't it?" I said, smiling from ear to ear.

"What exactly is this?" Jacob inquired.

I took a deep breath. "I'm starting a campaign – an anti-bullying awareness campaign." And so, my story began. I told the boys everything. The entire time I spoke, their eyes were locked and it was a relief to see that they were genuinely interested. From their reactions I could tell they'd be two of my strongest supporters. As I babbled on and on, I thought back to times during my darkest days when Mom or Dad would come into my room and let me know who had phoned. Marcel and Jacob were always on the list and yet I hadn't returned a single call to either one of them. I felt badly for Marcel because I'd blocked and barricaded our friendship, and for Jacob because I'd completely abandoned what was an exciting and intimate first love. Today it became inherently obvious that I wasn't the only one who'd been suffering over the last few months. It was now time to say what I knew needed to be said.

"Guys," I took an emotional pause. "I just want to tell you how sorry I am. I eliminated you both from my life and I realize how awful that is. But I need you to understand that these have been the worst and scariest months of my life. Shutting myself off was the only way I knew how to cope. I know 'sorry' doesn't cut it, but still, I need you to know that I really am."

While they didn't say or do much, I could tell that my apology meant something.

I switched gears hoping to move the conversation forward, "So, what do you think about the campaign?" I asked, eager to hear their opinions.

"You know what," I was surprised to hear Jacob quickly chime in to give his thoughts on the matter, "this is amazing, Kaitlyn. It's – it's just unbelievably inspiring and I can't wait for you to get it all out there. How are you going to start?"

Thrilled by his enthusiasm, I quickly answered, "Well, first I was thinking I'd begin talking to other students. I want to understand what other people are going through. I know that's easier said than done because it will take time for me to gain the trust of other students, but I think my story will help. And I know that Rebecca wasn't the only bully victim around here. I'm determined to find out more and I think in time, I'll get there."

"I think you're right," Jacob continued, "Chantel and her little clique–" his face erupted with an expression of sheer disgust, "it just doesn't make sense that Rebecca was their only target."

"Exactly," I went on. "I'm also going to talk to Principal Cabello later today to see if I can get permission to set up a booth in the open atrium over there during my spare period. I want to open a discussion table where people can come to learn more about what I'm doing, and pick up free t-shirts and other paraphernalia in production as we speak."

"Oh, Kaitlyn," Marcel piped up and then paused, seeming quite speechless on the matter. "Wow..." he trailed off.

I giggled.

The bell rang. 9:00am. Class had begun.

"I really have to go," I said, grabbing my bag and standing up from the table. "I certainly can't miss any more school!" I exclaimed, jokingly. We shared a brief laugh and then quickly went our separate ways to class.

21

THE STORY UNFOLDS

"**D**o you know someone who was bullied or who is being bullied now?" I asked softly.

The girl looked sheepishly into my eyes but then quickly shifted her glance away. It was clear she wanted to tell me something, and yet she was hesitant, looking as though she was almost afraid to speak.

I paused for a moment and watched her bite her lip and slide her index finger back and forth across the edge of the table that stood between us. Choosing my words wisely, I spoke again, "It's okay. I know how hard it is to admit that something wrong is happening. It's scary. But, bullying is even scarier. If we don't talk about it and share our stories and create awareness, it will take more of our friends' lives. I promise I won't judge you or make you feel badly about whatever it is that you want to say."

Again, the girl made eye contact and this time it stuck. For a moment, we looked at one another in silence. Then the girl opened her mouth and let out a sigh before saying, "It's about Rebecca."

My heart stood still. My lips separated in shock. "Okay," I said as calmly as possible, doing my best not to let the apprehensions of what I was feeling on the inside show in my voice. "Please tell me."

"You don't have an Instagram or Facebook account, do you?" the girl asked.

Confused by the question, I wondered the relevance of it. "No, why?" The truth of the matter was that prior to Rebecca's death, I really didn't have the time for it. I spent nearly every weekday evening at the dance studio and if there was something hilarious or outrageous on one of the platforms, someone always seemed to show me at school. And once I hit rock bottom in my bedroom, social media was the last thing on my mind.

"Right, I didn't think so because I searched your name and never found it," the girl began to explain, "And no one ever told you what was happening online?"

"Umm..." Now I was really puzzled. "No...what do you mean? What are you talking about?"

Again, she sighed. "Rebecca wasn't only bullied at school. It was happening online too."

My heart began to pound through my rib cage. I held my hand to my chest and muttered, "Nooo..."

"I know it must be hard to hear," the girl kept talking. Half of me wanted her to continue but the other half dreaded each new word she spoke. "Rebecca was so great. She and I weren't exactly close, but we sat next to one another in social studies class and we joked around and helped each other with projects. But then around October I think it was, she added me to Insta and Facebook. And–" she stopped and swallowed, her face all scrunched up at the thought of what was obviously a terrible memory. "And what was posted on her Facebook feed was awful...just so, so awful."

"What? What was it? What did people post there? And who posted? Was it Chantel? Or other people too?" I spewed out the questions fast, unable to contain myself.

The girl seemed a little startled. "It was all Chantel. But there were other kids liking her comments."

"Liking her comments?" I repeated, confused.

"Yeah, you can like people's comments on Facebook. So, Chantel was the name I always saw writing stuff to Rebecca but lots of other people would like Chantel's comments to her, and a few times there were comments from other people, sort of adding to what Chantel said. And then on Insta, Chantel and a couple others would constantly post offensive, mean things and tag her in them."

"Ugh," I let out a sigh of disgust. "How long did this go on for? Is it still online now?"

"I think so," the girl answered.

I'm not sure whether I was relieved or scared in that moment. Immediately I noticed she held a tablet underneath her left arm. I subtly pointed to the device and asked, "Will you show me?"

The question made her even more uncomfortable than she already was, "Oh, I don't...I don't know."

"Please," I pleaded with her. "This is something I need to see, no matter how hard it is."

Reluctantly, she pulled out the tablet from beneath her arm and opened the lid on her case. She touched the screen a few times and then turned the tablet to face me.

There it was. Rebecca's Facebook account. The first thing that struck me was her profile picture because it was exactly the same picture I had on the back of my t-shirt! The girl quickly picked up on my blank, confused stare and made her way around to the other side of the table to help me navigate through the social networking haven so foreign to me. She swiped down the web page to take us back in time.

"Are you sure you want to see this?" She asked again, continuing to swipe her finger up the screen.

"Yes, I'm sure."

Then she planted her finger flat in the middle of the screen and paused to verify the date. October 22nd. "Okay, it starts around here," she said.

I pulled the tablet a little closer and began reading. The comments started out in a taunting manner and progressively worsened as the days went on. The first few were strictly from Chantel, but as the girl explained, even though she was the instigator, many others participated in the evil act on a more secondary level. As I scrolled down in horror, I became puzzled by the fact that the comments suddenly stopped. I looked over at the girl, waiting for an explanation. Instantly, she knew exactly what I was thinking.

"This is only one outlet," She began, without even waiting for me to ask. "There are lots of other sites that were used to bully Rebecca."

"*Lots*?" I repeated in disbelief.

The girl didn't answer but quickly grabbed the tablet out of my hands and began finger tapping and swiping to take me to the next source. Unfortunately, I was even more ill prepared for what came next. It was a website – a full-fledged, live-online website. I couldn't believe it. Someone actually took the time to buy a domain name, design it and put it up on the Internet all to bully a fellow student? Pathetic.

A million thoughts raced through my mind as I wondered whether Chantel had gotten help from anyone to put such a disgraceful site online… maybe the others who accompanied her on the day of Rebecca's fatal beating…or had she done it herself? In huge black, capital letters across the top, it read: "SHE'S A LOSER". Blown up in the center of the website below the title was a rather unflattering picture of Rebecca. It was clear that someone had caught her in an awkward moment – probably without her even knowing a picture had been taken. Extending outwards from the picture were arrows pointing to specific parts of her face and body each with its own corresponding hateful remark. I winced in discomfort as I read through each bubble's content. From her hair, to her eyes, to her clothing, to her shoes, the comments ripped her to pieces. A tear streamed down my right cheek but I quickly swiped it away as I placed the tablet down on the table in front of me and stared outwards into the cafeteria which was now packed with people.

"Are you okay?" the girl's voice was soft and comforting.

"Oh, yes," I responded, trying my best not to alarm her. I wanted her to tell me everything she knew. "I'm not sure what I was expecting…it's just so terrible."

"I know. Maybe it would have been best if I didn't show you this?"

"No, no, no," I said with assurance. "I'm so grateful you came to talk to me. This is what my campaign is all about – speaking out – whether it's about Rebecca, you, or anyone else. It's hard for me to see all that, though."

"I know," she agreed, as her eyes dropped to the floor. A few seconds later she lifted them again and said, "I think it's really great…what you're doing, that is. And I'm so sorry about Rebecca. Even though I didn't know you before today, I saw you both together often at the beginning of school, and it was pretty clear how close you were. I can't imagine what you must be going through."

"Thank you, I really appreciate that. What's your name?" I asked the stranger.

"Karen," she answered.

"Kaitlyn," I replied, reaching my hand across my body to shake hers.

We shook and exchanged smiles. There was a pause as we sat in silence for a brief moment. Reluctant to ask for fear of what I knew she'd say, I inquired, "Is there a lot more?"

She frowned and replied, "Some...yeah."

I sighed, "Okay, please show me. I need to know."

Karen picked up her tablet from the table and again began her routine of touching and swiping her finger up and down the screen. "I'll show you everything I know about but I'm sure there are even text messages, online chats and emails that were private that we don't have access to."

I knew she was right. She took me to the next cyber bullying display, and then the next, and the next, and the next. As awful as it was, I battled my way through it, reading the horrible remarks on a slew of social media outlets and mini websites. And to think, it was all executed with the sole purpose of bullying this one, random, innocent individual.

As we continued, a terrible thought began to brew in my mind. Marcel! He surely would have known about this! And yet, he never spoke a word about it. How could he? How could he not tell me, not come to me with such critical information? Maybe it was *this* that drove Rebecca into the wretched depths of self-harm. Maybe it was the perpetual, persistent and relentless cyber bullying that slowly sucked the life out of her, that made her push away from the friendships, the intimacy and the love in her life. My face began to flush and my body grew hot as my anxiety mounted. I needed to speak to Marcel, and I needed to do it now.

His face was white with shock. With wide eyes, he looked at me, pausing for a moment before he spoke. "I should have known you'd find out."

My jaw dropped in disbelief. "*That's* your response? *That's* what you have to say to me, you jerk!?"

At once, his tone changed and it took me aback. "You know what? I'm not going to sit here and take this guilt trip from you, of all people!"

"Excuuuse me?" I was stunned by the accusatory nature of the words he spoke.

"Oh, give me a break, Kaitlyn! You actually have the nerve to come here and drill me on this? As if you don't understand? As if you have absolutely no idea why I might have kept this information to myself?!" He paused as if he were waiting for me to answer what I thought was most certainly a rhetorical question.

"Uh–" I stuttered.

"Why didn't YOU speak out about the first day of school? Why didn't YOU speak out about the incident between the lockers?!"

"Because–"

"Because she asked you not to!" There they were. The so obvious words of truth that I hadn't even considered before I'd questioned him. The revelation must have been written all over my face because Marcel then stood up straight, backed away a few steps and ran his hand through his hair. "She asked me not to."

I looked up at him, speechless.

"I wanted to tell you," Marcel continued, now a little more calmly. "But she pleaded with me and begged me and made me promise to keep my mouth shut. It was so hard. So unbelievably hard. It ate me up every day. At first, she showed me everything, and she cried and cried. At least then she was open about it. But after a while, she stopped. I think she knew how badly I wanted to tell someone, how much I wanted to put a stop to it. There were times when I would lie awake in bed at night and decide to myself that tomorrow would be the day when I'd tell – when I'd go against her persistent requests to stay quiet and get the help she needed. But then I'd wake up the next day and lose my will," he sighed deeply and then pressed on, "Oh Kaitlyn, I loved her so much…I was so in love with her. I was scared that if I broke my promise, I'd lose her. Towards the end, I could feel her slipping away and it totally freaked me out! At that point, there was no way I had any amount of courage to speak up…I was just doing everything I could to keep her happy, to show her how much I cared about her, to make her stay. And then–" He stopped suddenly and couldn't keep himself together any longer. Burying his face in his hands, he stood there and cried. I moved in and embraced him, showing him my support the only way I knew how. A few moments later he finished his sentence, "And then it was too late."

22

WHEELS IN MOTION

M y palms were cold and sweaty and I kept rubbing my hands together
to try and keep them dry. I tapped my right foot nervously as I
watched the students file into the gym. No notes, no cue cards – I knew
what I wanted to say and I was well aware of the fact that I'd totally lose
my audience if I read from a piece of paper. This topic called for more than
scribbled notes; it needed to come from the heart. How would they react?
What would their responses be like? Would anyone care at all? Would I be
able to maintain my composure? Would I have enough emphasis to truly
resonate with my crowd?

Time would tell.

"Are you ready, Kaitlyn?" Mr. Kemp stood to my left, joining me as I
watched the crowd grow larger still.

I looked over at him and smiled, "I'm ready." And I really was. Sure,
my nerves were uncontrollable but I had an air of confidence about me
that day. I believed so strongly in my purpose that everything else seemed
insignificant in comparison. I could only hope that my words and my

presentation were strong enough to make an impact. The school screamed for change. Over the last few weeks, I was astonished at the number of people who visited my campaign booth in the atrium, many of whom had bullying stories of their own. Sometimes it was the victims themselves who reached out to me and other times it was bystanders speaking on behalf of a friend. My atrium campaigning taught me one thing if not a thousand: as much as she felt as though she were, Rebecca was far from alone.

I'd structured my campaign around the bystander – not the victim. I believed that, in the vast majority of cases, the bystander (or bystanders) could do *more*. The presentation I was about to give targeted those very people, illustrating through Rebecca's story, that their decisions can have a profound effect on a situation's outcome.

"Okay, Kaitlyn. Everyone is seated now. We're about two minutes to start time," Principal Cabello instructed me.

"Great, thanks," I took a deep breath. "Everything is functional with the projector screen?"

"Yep," he answered. "We've got your cover slide up now and here's the remote control. Simply click this button to move forward to the next slide. And here's your mic."

"Perfect," I responded, feeling my stomach flip upside down as I realized just how close we were to show time.

A moment later Principal Cabello's voice came one last time. "Okay, Kaitlyn. Whenever you're ready."

And with that, I pressed my shoulders back, tilted my chin up and walked out to the center of the gymnasium. It was phenomenally loud as the buzz of students' voices echoed through the large space. As I took the stage, I wondered how I would possibly get them quiet without saying "hello" or some other lame greeting into the mic. I didn't want to ruin the effect of my carefully planned opening. Turns out I didn't have to because the more steps I took, the quieter the gym became and by the time I arrived in the center, there were only a few straggling voices remaining. Confidence took over. I commanded the stage. I stood there, my mic dangling down by my side and stared straight ahead. No words were necessary. After about 30 seconds, the entire gymnasium, filled with just shy of two thousand students and teachers, was silent.

I slowly drew the mic up to my mouth.

"Silence kills," I took a long pause and scanned the audience from left to right. I had their attention. "It doesn't seem like it at the time. After all, *you* aren't the one doing it. *You* aren't the one making hateful remarks. *You* aren't the one hiding behind a computer screen making someone else's life a living hell. And it isn't *you* who decided to take it to the next level and get physical." Again, I paused. I wanted every single word to sink in. I spoke slowly…authoritatively.

"But it *was* you. It *is* you.

"For me, it's no consolation that *I* wasn't the one who beat Rebecca Blaine in the schoolyard of Leacrest High." Without a flinch, I clicked the button below my index finger to change the slide on the projector screen behind me. I didn't turn around to check, but the gasps from my audience told me my image displayed. It was of Rebecca in the hospital just one day after she was admitted and disturbing to say the least. "This is my best friend you're looking at, just two days before she died. It wasn't me who did this to her. And I suppose, since that's the case, then I shouldn't feel responsible, right? But I do. And why is that? Why is it that I battled post traumatic stress disorder and clinical depression for two and a half months after she was taken from me? Because I *do* feel responsible. And so I should. The truth of the matter is, I saw it. I watched it happen. I hid, cowardly behind a tree where I saw every punch…every kick…every blow to her face and body. Those images continue to haunt me every second, of every minute, of every day," I swallowed hard as I fought back tears. I knew I had to stay strong for my audience. The effectiveness of my campaign depended on it.

"No matter how close of a relationship you have with someone, you may not know everything about them. Is this person happy? Sad? Are they struggling with something in their life? Do you know what they did after school yesterday or what kind of a relationship they have with their parents at home?

"I thought I knew everything there was to know about my best friend, Rebecca Blaine. I know that on the first day of school, a girl confronted Rebecca outside of the school cafeteria. Claiming that Rebecca had shoved her in the lineup, the girl began to intimidate and badger my friend. I know that on November 22nd, her bully attacked again and Rebecca was choked and slammed against the lockers just outside the atrium. I know now that the day after this incident, Rebecca was distant towards me and that this was the day when she began to disengage herself from our friendship. I know that two days later, I met her at a local coffee shop in our neighborhood and I felt relieved that she'd agreed to come. I thought we'd talk about our next step – about what we were going to do to stop her bully from making another move. I know that Rebecca asked me not to tell anyone and made me promise to keep this information to myself. I know that I listened. I know that on March 22nd, Rebecca was brutally beaten in the schoolyard of Leacrest High. I know that the next few days of my life were the scariest days I've ever experienced and yet still, I had no comprehension of the fact that she might not make it. I know that on March 25th, my very best friend, a beautiful, funny, talented, honest, fun-loving girl died of an ischemic stroke at North Lake Hospital. I know that my silence killed her – at least in part. And I know that for the next two and a half months,

I battled a dark mental state so severe that I felt unworthy of living if she couldn't live too.

"What I didn't know was that this wasn't nearly the full story. I didn't know Rebecca was not only bullied at school but also online. I didn't know that for months, since the very first day of school, her bullies never relented – Facebook, online chat rooms, mobile text messages, even mini websites were created to insult, humiliate and degrade her. I didn't know that she cut herself. I didn't know that she resorted to self-harm because it was the only way she knew how to cope. I didn't know she started to withdraw from the world and that it wasn't only me she was avoiding but also her family and her boyfriend, who I know she loved so much. I didn't know that my best friend was suffering. I didn't know that life had become so difficult – that it had gotten so bad.

"On November 10th, what if I'd said 'no' at that coffee shop? What if I hadn't promised Rebecca that I'd keep her secrets? What if I'd followed my gut instinct and gone to someone for help? Maybe I wouldn't be standing here in front of you today. Maybe Rebecca would still be here. I know it's scary. Bullies are intimidating and they are capable of irreparable damage. But they are few and we are many. However, the power of our collective group means nothing if we stay silent. If we are bystanders, we are part of the crime. We let it happen, we make it possible and we perpetuate future occurrences. Just the same way we allowed it, together, we have the power to stop it. One bully can't take down an entire bus full of kids. One bully can't get up if everyone else pushes them down. One bully can't insult and offend people if no one's listening.

"As bystanders, we have what the bully doesn't – strength in numbers. No matter how many bullies there are in a school, there will always be more of us. It takes confidence. It takes strength and it takes courage. But for the sake of our Rebeccas, for the sake of our best friends, our sisters, our brothers and our classmates, we must break the silence. The worst thing we can do is refuse to learn from our mistakes. We will screw up, we will face bad times, and we will wish we'd acted differently in past situations. The question is not what we could have done to change the outcome of past events but rather what will we do when it happens again? Will we repeat our mistake? Will we forget how much we regretted the way we acted the first time? Will we hide behind our doubts and fears and let the bully win yet again?

"In the case of Rebecca Blaine, the students who brutally beat her in our school yard are expelled from school and facing charges. Is that any way to live your adolescent life? I'm almost certain those kids had no idea what their punches and kicks were capable of. Sure, they obviously wanted to make a statement, to rough her up. But little did they know that all it took was one, fluke hit to the side of her temple that caused severe bleeding around her brain…and eventually, death. As I stand here, I'm no idiot. I know not all of you sitting here today are bystanders. Some of you are victims. Some of you are bullies. If you're a bully, let me ask you, *why*? Do you enjoy seeing others' misery? Does it make you feel better to put someone else down? Is your life so horrible that you have to make others' lives horrible too? Are your teenaged insecurities so deep that you feel like there's no other way to cope with your negative sense of self than to insult, degrade and hurt other people? And where does it end? At what point do you decide you've gone too far? Is it when you're called into the principal's office? When your victim's parents call yours? When you're reported to the police? When a death occurs…? What is your limit? Or do you even have one?

"In the future, when you're in your twenties, how will you feel when you look back on the type of person you were in high school? If you seriously hurt or even killed someone, what kind of a life will you have made for yourself? How will you be experiencing what many say are the best years of your life? Now imagine yourself in your thirties. You have kids of your own and your entire perspective on life changes. Now you're in your forties. It's the first day of high school for your son or daughter. How will it make you feel to be fearful of the fact that there may be a bully – a bully exactly like you – just waiting to get their hands on your little boy or girl. Imagine your adolescent child going through what you put so many others through.

"And now ask yourself, is it really worth it? Whatever thrill you're getting out of the experience now – is it worth a serious injury, the destruction of someone's self-confidence, a suicide or a death?

"In honor of Rebecca Blaine, it's time for Leacrest to take a stand. It's time for change. We've all read the articles and heard the newscasts. Bullying is an evil social epidemic. It calls for serious action and it calls for it right now. Right this minute. Can you feel the change in YOU?

"Change starts with one tiny little step that you make. While that's definitely true, this very problem calls for a collective change. If we want to make a statement and create real change, we need to do it together as a school, as a community, as a collective group of people that fuels the power of the individual to create a team that's impossible to stop.

"Together... Let's save the self-esteem of the person sitting next to you. Let's save the confidence of the quiet guy in your math class. Let's save the tears of the eccentric girl who dresses differently from the rest of us. Let's save the life of the student who doesn't deserve to die.

"I don't plan to stand up here once. I'll be here several more times after this. Change is about talking, communicating and being open with each other. My campaign has only just begun. I want to thank you all for your time here today and I'll be standing here, right in this very spot for a long time afterwards, hoping you'll come talk to me. Tell me your stories.

Tell me your feelings. Tell me your ideas about how we can make tomorrow different.

"Make a commitment to yourselves. To be someone better. To be someone braver. To be someone who isn't afraid to stand up. Open your mouth. Because it's *Time to Talk*."

23

TO MY DELIGHTED SURPRISE

Silence filled the space. I stood there, confidently, not moving an inch. One, two, three seconds went by. Nothing. Nobody moved. My heart began to race and my stomach flipped upside down. Was it too short? Too long? Was I not loud enough? Did I not say the right things? Did I not get through to anyone? They didn't like it...

And then, my fellow students made a gesture. One by one, they began to clap. Loud. Within a few seconds, the entire audience was on their feet clapping, howling and whistling in approval. It was an indescribable feeling and one that I don't know I'll ever be able to replicate again in my lifetime. The noise echoed through my body and I didn't feel alone anymore. Beginning on that very day, Rebecca lived on.

The crowd stood there applauding me for what felt like an eternity and then something even more incredible happened. I began to notice movement over to the right. There was a girl making her way down the bleachers, weaving in and out of the people in her path. At first, I paid no mind, thinking she simply wanted to leave. But instead of walking out the gymnasium doors to her left, she began to walk diagonally to her right – towards me! I looked over and smiled at her as she came closer and closer with each step. As the crowd became aware of the girl, they grew quiet. I don't quite think the girl was prepared for that and she seemed startled by the silence. But she was quick on the draw and reached her hand towards the microphone in my left. Looking straight at me, she asked politely, "May I?"

I nodded in agreement.

She looked at the audience and in a booming and authoritative voice, bellowed the words, "I'm up here to talk to Kaitlyn about *my* experiences with bullying. You should do the same."

And you know what? They did. Left, right and middle – they came from all angles. Students began to break away from the crowd and make their way to the center of the gymnasium where we stood. Before I knew it, a massive circle of people surrounded me. The girl who started it all looked at me and smiled, "I'm Jocelyn," she said, reaching out her hand.

I shook it firmly. "Kaitlyn," I responded. "Thank you for what you did."

"Thank *you*," she said kindly in return.

And with that, the conversation began. She told me of her battles with bullying and about how difficult it was for her to feel good about herself. Jocelyn even brought up the names of individuals who had bullied her. It was incredible. Although I could tell that it was hard for her to speak about it, there was a frustrated determination about her. She had sternness and vigor in her voice. As she named off her hated bullies, other kids in the crowd chimed in, "She bullied me too!" and, "Oh, him? Yeah, he was harassing me on the bus last week!" and, "Oh, I can't stand her!"

It was everything I could have hoped for: open, honest communication that signaled the start of something real – something powerful. These quiet, scared and insecure teenagers were speaking up! Their assertive no-nonsense attitudes were palpable. We stood there for the better part of an hour, talking, venting and getting it all out – and the support we received from one another was truly inspiring. There were even bystanders who shared the same guilt and regret that I did. In that hour, the fifty or sixty of us who stood there realized something very important: we weren't alone. As soon as one of us shared something that made us feel vulnerable, another crowd member immediately agreed and added to the comment. It was as though years of bottled up information and internal torment was set free. We were liberated. We were together. And little did we know that we were on the verge of something truly amazing.

After that day, *Time to Talk* took off. Every day during my two spare periods, I set up a booth in the atrium where students could come to talk, to give me their ideas, to join my campaign and to buy various awareness products that I'd put together. There were t-shirts, pins, ribbons, bracelets and phone cases. The color was yellow and as the weeks went by, the response at Leacrest was astounding. I kept a tally of how many people visited my booth, how many joined my campaign and how many bought awareness items. The numbers grew daily. Gradually, the color yellow flooded our school. Not only did students buy the awareness items, but they actually wore them! Every single day, a little more yellow could be seen popping up here and there amidst the crowds. As students walked by my booth, they'd point to their t-shirts, show me their ribbons and flash their bracelets in support. I'd smile and give a thumbs up. I couldn't believe what was happening. Although Rebecca's death still haunted me, and although there wasn't a single moment that went by where I didn't miss my dear friend, the campaign gave me a sense of comfort – a feeling of purpose. If

I couldn't be with her, the campaign at least allowed me the opportunity to honor her name and to use her story as a driving force for change.

And I saw the change. Every day, there was a little more progression. But the real pivotal moment that signified meaningful and powerful change, came in a different form. After almost one month, I began to plan my next rally. I spoke to Principal Cabello and scheduled a date exactly one month after my first. I figured this was a good schedule – just enough time had passed and yet not too much that people had completely forgotten. For *Time to Talk* it was clear that momentum was critical. This time, I had a team behind me. Marcel was my righthand man, and ten other students had joined our campaign to help generate new awareness initiatives – one of whom, was Jocelyn Parker who I thought to be a brilliant writer at the young age of 16. Jocelyn began to produce articles about our anti-bullying efforts and contacted various media outlets in the area. Personally, I thought it was a long shot, but she was determined. She'd report back regularly, telling us which news companies she'd sent her articles to, and what television channels she'd contacted. Every week, our school newspaper would feature one of her articles and Jocelyn would keep the newsletter, frame the article and display them at our booth in the atrium.

Several days before our second rally, as a few us were campaigning at our booth in the atrium, there was an announcement for me to visit the office. I simply assumed it was Principal Cabello who wanted to give me some input for the rally or confirm our equipment needs. Entering quite nonchalantly, I walked through to his office with a warm greeting, "Hi there," I said cheerfully, as I plunked myself in the chair opposite his desk.

"Hi, Kaitlyn," he smiled. "How are the preparations coming along for the rally on Friday?"

"Good," I said. "We've got some great participants to tell their stories and we've actually put together a slide show of a few powerful illustrations of bullying events that have taken place right at our school like Facebook posts, screenshots of text messages, and even kids who've taken photos of bruises and other markings they've received from bullies."

"Okay," he answered. "But 'good' isn't going to cut it this time."

I furrowed my brow, almost defensively, "What do you mean?"

"Well, you're going to have to be great," he said with a grin from ear to ear, and then paused before saying, "because this time you're going to have a few special guests in your audience."

"Oh," I said, confused. "Who?"

"Manis TV, Rock Air and the City Post."

My eyes lit up as I bounced straight out of the chair, "Are you serious?!" I exclaimed.

"Very much so," he said with a little chuckle.

I screeched in delight as I jumped up from my chair. "Oh, thank you!"

He laughed again, "Don't thank me. Thank yourself – and that campaigner of yours, Jocelyn Parker."

"We've got to get to work!" I said, jumping up from my seat with excitement. As I made my way to the door, I looked back for a second. "Mr. Cabello, don't worry. We'll be great."

He gave me a look of admiration and replied, "I have no doubt."

With that, I walked speedily out of his office and ran down to the atrium to tell the group. Two of the largest local television broadcast companies and the city's largest newspaper! I felt as though I might explode. "Guys, guys!" I yelled, still at least 30 feet away from them. They all looked up from the table in unison. "You'll never guess what's happening!" I exclaimed, barely able to contain myself. "Manis TV, Rock Air and City Post are attending our rally on Friday!" Reacting much the same way I had, the group squealed in delight and began jumping up and down with excitement.

"Are you serious??" Jocelyn questioned.

"Yes, and it's all thanks to you!" I answered, giving her a huge hug. Then I grabbed her shoulders and looked her straight in the eyes, "Thank you, thank you, thank you for believing in us and for working so hard to get our voices heard."

She smiled from ear to ear. "Kaitlyn, we wouldn't be here without you. And now we actually have a real shot at not only helping the kids in our own school but maybe others too!"

We huddled close together and enjoyed the moment. And what a terrific moment it was. Thrilling, motivating and so, so exciting. True to form, after a few seconds of relishing in our triumph we began brainstorming about how we could make Friday's rally even more impactful.

The reporters sat in the first row of bleachers to the right side. Video cameras were left and right. A sea of yellow filled the stands. The twelve of us stood, center stage in the middle of the gymnasium. I breathed slowly and took it all in. The mic in front of me, I began to speak. Here goes nothing.

"Who's no longer silent?" I yelled out to the crowd. Immediately they responded with a powerful, loud cheer. My heart melted with pride as I let the energy take me over. I paused, waiting for the gym to grow quiet again. Showtime.

For the next 45 minutes, my team and I took our attentive audience through a series of touching stories, told by bullies, bystanders and victims at Leacrest High. Not only did they speak of their actions and experiences in the past, but they also told the students how they had made real, daily efforts to change in the last month. Some were campaigners and others were guest speakers who had agreed to tell their most heart wrenching experiences to the audience. In between each story, we asked motivational questions and spoke of change. We played slide shows and videos that brought tears to the eyes of many attendees. We prompted questions and open conversation from audience members to speak up. For power, impact and branding consistently, we ended the same way I'd ended my first presentation.

I stepped up to the microphone to finish.

"Make a commitment to yourselves. To be someone better. To be someone braver. To be someone who isn't afraid to stand up. Open your mouth. Because it's **Time to Talk**."

This time there was no pause from the crowd. As one collective group, they jumped to their feet and erupted in a cheer that swept us off our feet. We smiled and stood up together, holding hands. The rush was more than words could ever describe. As the applause continued, I looked back at the projector screen behind us. There she was…Rebecca. I smiled at her and turned back around as a tear streamed down my face. We'd done it. I could feel the success of our presentation oozing out every crevice of the gymnasium. After a few minutes, a sea of students traveled towards us, ready to talk – and we were ready to listen. The rest is almost a blur. I spoke with many students that day – brand new faces that had since built up the courage to come forward and speak about their experiences and feelings. Some came up just to tell us how moved they were by our rally and others just wanted to hear what everyone else had to say. No matter what their purpose, it was their presence that was most powerful.

After a while the crowd began to disperse and as I finished my conversations with the last few students, I noticed that our visitors were still there. I wasn't sure how long we'd been speaking to our fellow student body but I was surprised to see that they hadn't left. When it was just the twelve of us left in the middle of the gymnasium, I saw Principal Cabello and Mr. Kemp usher the media over to us. Cameras and all, the group of them walked in our direction. I tapped Marcel so he'd turn around to see what was about to happen. He stopped his conversation, looked at me and then looked at them and smiled.

A lady with long blonde hair stood out front and said to us, "That was truly incredible. I'm interested in doing a feature spot of your campaign on our network. We're wondering if it might be alright for us to conduct a group interview with all of you."

I quickly spoke up, "Absolutely."

"Okay, so let's set up a few chairs right here in a semicircle and have you all sit down together," the lady immediately got down to business.

Smiling from ear to ear, we keenly followed her instructions. It was as though we had become instant celebrities. I felt such pride for my group that day. We settled from the excitement of the rally and were calm, confident and well spoken – despite the butterflies I know we all felt in the pit of our stomachs. We let ourselves be vulnerable, staying true to our open and honest mantra. It was a gripping, heartfelt and emotional interview. The reporters' questions had depth and it was nice to be able to speak without fear, shame or doubt. We knew that if any part of this was to air on television, it would need to be something special. And apparently it was. Because we earned featured spots on both television stations, and a significant article in the city newspaper.

Word spread. Fast. In the weeks and months following, Principal Cabello was flooded with phone calls from other schools in surrounding areas with requests for presentations and rallies from our group. I even scheduled *Time to Talk* to present at Hope Hills Public School where I had reported the act of bullying among the boys at recess. Our Facebook, Instagram and Twitter following hit nearly five digits over the course of a few months. We were inundated by emails from parents, students and fellow community members. At school, we were practically celebrities. And although we continued to sit at our booth twice a day, visits from students had drastically changed. Our guests no longer came to speak about their awful experiences, but rather about positive, enlightened stories – a bully who apologized, a bystander who stood up or a courageous effort on the part of the storyteller.

There was a transformation at work. Bullies stopped being bullies and bystanders stopped standing on the sidelines. Students were happier and friendlier towards one another.

We raised more money and attracted more campaigners. Our voice was growing. We were being heard. We were actually helping people.

Who knows how many kids we'd already influenced. Who knows where we'd end up next. Although the future held uncertainty, there's one thing that was undoubtedly true: our voice was getting louder. How interesting it was to me that on the sunny day at the antique store, something clicked. I realized how critical it was for me to break my silence.

The only way out of my debilitating mental state was, quite simply, to realize it was *Time to Talk.*

The only way out for that boy in the schoolyard of Hope Hills was for me to have enough gumption to tell myself it was *Time to Talk.*

And today, right now, this very minute, the only way out for Leacrest, for Hope Hills, for public schools, high schools, communities and the people who inhabit them is to know in their hearts that it is *Time to Talk.*

This is the key. The starting point for alteration.

But Rebecca didn't know. She thought differently. Perhaps she was stuck. Afraid. Alone. In pain. She thought the only way out was a desperate attempt to gain some form of control and comfort through isolation and self-harm. And it was to her heartbreaking demise, which came far too soon.

It took the strike of tragedy for change to occur.

Now, it was up to us to be different. To break out of the horror and speak up. *Time to Talk*. Once we do it for ourselves, it then becomes our responsibility to guide others. And that's exactly what the campaign is all about.

After only a few months, it's already apparent. Undeniable, in fact. Intense, motivational and contagious.

We're on to something.

Could it be? Is it possible? Would we be the movement society needed us to be? It's up to me to believe.

She couldn't do it for herself, but in time, Rebecca, oh my incredible Rebecca will do it for others. She'll make her mark on the world with her story. A story so powerful that it deeply and meaningfully impacts the people who hear it. The message is in the story. Not a shred of doubt remains.

There *is* a way out. But there's only one.

Recognizing.

Knowing.

Trusting.

Believing.

It's *Time to Talk*.